COUNTRY GIRL
BY THE CREEK

COUNTRY GIRL
BY THE CREEK

LINDA HABECK

authorHOUSE®

AuthorHouse™
1663 Liberty Drive
Bloomington, IN 47403
www.authorhouse.com
Phone: 1-800-839-8640

Published by AuthorHouse 11/06/2014

ISBN: 978-1-4969-5152-6 (sc)
ISBN: 978-1-4969-5151-9 (e)

Library of Congress Control Number: 2014919879

DEDICATION

---◆---

This is dedicated to my children, Jennifer, Jana and Jacob, who were my inspirations in writing; And to my Husband Scott, who has always stood by my side, in whatever I do.

CHAPTER ONE

✦

Life was harder without Papa home. Mamma and the children had to do all the chores and the things that papa always did. Papa knew if he didn't find a job, they would lose their homestead. They had to pay the land taxes. Mr. Smith was not only the president of the bank, he also made sure that all county residents paid their taxes, or their homesteads would go back to the state, and other families could apply for them. So papa went away to find work; as there was nothing to be found in Crawford County. That was six weeks ago, and Mamma hadn't heard from him yet. Mamma knew how long that the 'U.S. Mail' could take, and it could be a long time to get through; so she didn't act worried, but they all knew better. She had Pauline check with the post-mistress everyday after school to see if there was a letter from papa. Pauline knew how to do this, as they had gotten letters from her Grandparents in the past, and besides she '*was*' almost sixteen.

Mamma had Pauline check, because if she sent one of the boys, they might end up at the creek fishing, or looking for toads. The boys worked hard at their chores, but they were not as responsible as Pauline. Of course Pauline was older, and she didn't care to look for toads because she thought they were gross. Her brothers would sometimes bring toads home, and tease Pauline with them. Mamma would say, *"Pauline dear, that's just what boys do. Ignore them and they'll quit",* but of course they didn't. She often thought they were too immature, but 'boys will be boys'.

Mamma and Papa talked before he left; when he found work, he would send word that he was ok, and also send money to pay on the land taxes. They would be able to buy any necessities they needed, and maybe new shoes and material for clothes, if there was any money left over. Pauline knew in her heart, that there wouldn't be, but she could always wish. She was always dreaming and wishing about something, she was always thinking of things to do or to make. Mamma could tell when she was daydreaming by the far off look in Pauline's eyes. There was a beautiful bolt of material at Mrs. Kramer's store that she would love to have to make a new Sunday dress. It had little pink roses, petite green leaves, all on a soft yellow background; and she could make a bonnet and a purse to match. Mamma could make a pattern for a dress right out her head. Pauline was sure, that if she could ever afford the material, mamma would help make a wonderful pattern, which would enhance Pauline's youthful figure.

Pauline was tired after working at Mrs. Kramer's and doing her chores and didn't want to do her school work. Pauline was to milk the cow twice a day, until the cow died. She also was supposed to help mamma in the kitchen, make the beds, and other simple tasks. She had worked an hour and a half at Mrs. Kramer's, after school, sewing and doing alterations. Mrs. Kramer was a very nice lady and paid Pauline twenty five cents for every alteration, and a whole dollar for every whole garment she made. People actually ordered new clothes to be made. This was new to Pauline, as mamma had always made their clothes, at least until Pauline was old enough to sew her own. Mamma had shown her how to sew perfect stitches, which would hardly show. Mamma still helped Pauline with the patterns, as did Mrs. Kramer at "*Kramer's Dress Shoppe and Alterations*".

Pauline was trying to help mamma and papa, so they could pay the land taxes and not lose their home. She was old enough to know that they were having a hard time paying them, plus she had heard them talking one night about it, before papa left. Mamma was not happy about her working, but knew Pauline was right, they needed the money. Mamma was trying to keep the farm going while Papa was gone. They had twenty acres, if they could keep the farm going for five years, it would be theirs. They had eight acres for hay, and eight acres for corn. The rest was basically yard, garden and a small creek that wound through out the land. They had three more years to go, to keep the land farmed, and the land taxes paid. There would always be land taxes, but they had to maintain the farm until the five year mark, that was the agreement with the government. Other families had already given up, and moved into town or back east.

They had moved here two years ago, after Papa saw an ad in a paper, about land for homesteading. They were living in Illinois, in a logging camp. They had lived in a two room shack, near the big lake, and they had to pay rent for it. Papa worked in the logging camp, the work was hard and dangerous. The schooling there was not very good, and it depended on if the township could find a teacher. The "house" was small for all of them, and Pauline had to share a bed with her brothers. Emily slept in her cradle, but she had outgrown that a long time ago. The children's bed, doubled as sitting space during the day. There was a small cook stove, and the oven barely was big enough for one loaf of bread. The stove also was the only heat in the small house. Mamma had hung a sheet around her and papas bed, for a little privacy. The children took turns, in the mornings and at night, changing behind the 'curtain'.

The house was not nearly big enough for their family, and the children seemed to quarrel a lot. The logging camp was also not that big. The 'houses' were very close to each other, and one family could hear what was said in the neighbor's house. Mamma wanted more room and more privacy. Pauline could hear mamma cry a lot at night, and papa would always try to console her, and promised that he would look for something better.

Mamma and Papa wanted their own land, and Mamma wanted a larger house, with bedrooms, actual bedrooms that had walls. The land was in Minnesota, and papa had said it may get colder there in the winters, with more snow, but if mamma wanted to try to farm, they could go. Mamma agreed with papa, so they moved. Mamma remembered those winters from when they used to live in Minnesota, but it was too good to pass up. So they packed up what the wagon could carry, leaving enough room for the children. The cow could walk behind, tethered with a rope to the wagon. The chickens were put in a crate papa had made, that he had fastened to the bottom of the wagon and they set off for Minnesota, to the new homestead.

* * * * *

Mamma wanted their new house built by the creek. It was so pretty there, and handy for hauling water; they would have to use a bucket to haul the water to the house, as there wasn't a hand pump. It was also close enough for the children to play in the creek and mamma and papa could keep a close eye on them. Pauline was the oldest of four, and was almost sixteen. Peter was twelve, Matthew was eight and baby Emily was two. Mamma had also lost two babies, but they didn't talk about that much, as it made mamma cry.

There was a big oak tree in the front yard. Papa hung a rope for the children to swing on, and sometimes they would swing and jump right into the creek, all the children, except Emily of course. Peter and Matthew also liked to fish in the creek, and sometimes they caught enough fish, that mamma could fry them up for supper. Sometimes the boys would climb the big oak, or any of the other trees around their house. It was great to actually have a yard, without neighbors so close. The children barely quarreled now, since they had more room to move around and play, plus they had actual chores to keep them busy and school on a regular basis.

Mamma worked all day in the fields. She cut hay or cut the corn, until the children came home from school. Then she would make supper, Pauline always tried to help mamma. Emily played in the fields by Mamma except when she was napping. Pauline knew that mamma worked very hard, and wanted to help out as much as possible.

Supper wasn't always much; biscuits and flour gravy and sometimes even a little salt pork. The milk cow had died last winter, and they couldn't afford to get a new one, so for now there wasn't any milk, unless they bought it from a neighbor. Sometimes Mamma would put sugar in their water glasses, for a treat. Oh, and apple pies. Mamma made wonderful apple pies. The children would pick the apples from the five trees on their farm. They called it "The Little Orchard by the Creek", and maybe someday, there could be a sign over the dirt driveway leading to the house. Pauline was always dreaming, and she could envision a pole fence, with the sign over the pathway to their yard. She could paint apples on the sign, and paint "Mayfield's Orchard by the Creek".

Pauline begged Mamma to let her do her school work in the morning. Mamma didn't like this idea either, but gave into her, "*just this once*" she said. She knew how tired Pauline was. She had never seen black circles under her eyes like this before. Pauline had been staying up late at night, to make sure her chores and school work was finished. She made the beds in the mornings before school, except on the weekends, but mamma insisted they be made as early as possible, as mamma liked a neat house. Mamma really took pride in her new house, as it seemed so spacious after living in the shack by the lake. This house even had a wood floor, which was a treat for everyone in the family.

Peter helped a lot by raking the hay in the make-shift barn, for the horses, feeding the horses, and even working in the fields after school once in awhile. He wanted to be the man of the family with Papa away. He didn't want to go to school. He wanted to stay home and work in the fields during the day with Mamma. Mamma wouldn't hear of it. "*In this day and age, you need an education*", she would say. Peter knew mamma was right, and knew not to argue anymore.

Matthew mostly played. But he did bring in stove wood for Mamma every morning and every night. He would also feed the few chickens they had, and bring in the eggs, so at least they had fresh eggs in the mornings for breakfast. And salt toast, if Mamma had enough flour to make bread. Matthew also helped set the table for meals, and the three older children took turns washing the dishes.

Baby Emily just played and napped. She liked the pots and pans most, because they could make lots of noise if she pounded them on the wooden floor. She had a hand-me-down rag doll that was once Pauline's. Most of the stuffing was gone, and it was soiled and stained. Emily didn't care, as she called it *"baby"*. Pauline got up the next morning, and as promised, did her home work. She was up before the boys, and even hauled in the stove wood for Matthew. It was a beautiful day, and maybe today, mamma would hear from Papa, maybe Papa would say he was coming home. Pauline found her mind wandering again.

CHAPTER TWO

❖

Papa had built their new house, along with the help of some neighbors. Mamma, Pauline and the boys helped as much as possible. It was such a large house, compared to what they were used to. Mamma and papa had a bedroom downstairs, with walls and a curtain in the doorway. Papa built Emily a crib-like bed that fit her better. In the loft there was a wall separating Pauline's side from the boys' side. The boys still shared a bed, but now Pauline had a bed to herself. She knew that when Emily got a little older, she would have to share her bed with her, but for right now, she was enjoying her privacy. Of course, Pauline might be married and gone from the house, before baby Emily was old enough to move upstairs, she daydreamed.

Papa had built in a fireplace with a place to bake bread off to the side. In addition, there was a stove with a good sized oven. There was a sink that drained outside, but it would hold water for washing dishes, or bathing Emily. Mamma and papa had their own rocking chairs, and they each had a chair around the kitchen table. Emily sat in her high chair, but papa had made her a matching kitchen chair for when she got older. Life was so much easier in this new house.

It was a fall day and the leaves were changing colors to beautiful oranges, yellows and reds, and were falling in the breezes. Walking in the yard made a great rustle in the leaves, and if the children had enough free time, they could use the barn rake, and make leaf piles and jump in them. They could never do that in Illinois.

The time for picking berries was over, although mamma had canned some for preserves in the winter months. She made the best preserves, and they were even better on mamma's warm bread. Mamma was teaching Pauline how to make the breads, and other recipes. She hoped she could learn to cook as well as mamma, as Pauline thought mamma was the best cook in the world, and papa would often say so too. The more she helped mamma in the kitchen, the more she was learning.

Pauline was hoping Mamma would hear from Papa; that he had found work and would be sending money home. Or better yet, he was coming home. Mamma sure looked tired and worn out. Her hands were calloused and worn from working in the fields, sometimes they would even bleed. But she never complained and always seemed to be in a good mood. Pauline was learning how to cook, and was starting to help mamma make meals, so she could rest. Only once in a while did mamma get out of sorts, and the children knew to behave then, even Emily.

Pauline stopped at the post office after school everyday, hoping to get a letter from papa. This day was no different, *"Any mail for Mamma, Mrs. Davis?"* Mrs. Davis was the post-mistress.

"Yes, as a matter of fact there is, Dear. It is addressed to Mrs. Suza Mayfield.", Mrs. Davis said in her soft sweet voice. *"Mayfield"* she laughed, *"always makes me think of the new flowers swaying in the fields during the spring breezes. I guess we will have to wait for spring now, to see those flowers. Oh here child, here is the letter. I get to chatting and forget what I am doing"* and then she almost giggled.

Mrs. Davis was a widow, and she only took the job at the post office for something to do. Mr. Davis had left her a fortune when he passed away the year before, but she never treated people differently because they didn't have money. Mrs. Davis handed Pauline the envelope, "*I hope it is what your mamma has been waiting for*", and it was, it was a letter from Papa.

"*Oh, thank you, Mrs. Davis. I must get this home to Mamma*" she left running, and ran all the way home, forgetting about working for Mrs. Kramer. "*Mamma, Mamma*", she yelled as she got close to the house.

"*Slow down Dear. What is it?*"

Pauline couldn't catch her breath. "*A let. . . . Letter.... from Pa - pa*", she said panting.

Mamma could hardly get the letter open. She fumbled and fumbled, as her fingers were so sore from working. Finally she ripped open the end of the envelope.

"*Dear Suza.*" That's what Papa called Mamma, it was short for Suzanne. "*I am in Rochester. It is approximately 60 miles from home, and the train ride is almost an eight hour ride. I am working at a furniture factory. I am making six fifty a week. Six dollars and fifty cents, can you believe it? Now we should be able to keep the farm, I am sure.*"

"*Plus I can get a bonus if I put detail on the backs of chairs. I'm glad I brought my chisels with me. You said I should take them. Thank you Suza.*"

"*I should start sending money home next week. Also, I can come home every third weekend for three days. I can take the train. It costs fifty cents to ride home and back, if I take a regular seat. I can sleep there if I wish. That is if you think we can afford it. I will come home, and we will discuss it.*"

"*I miss all of you, and hope to be home for good by Christmas. We should have enough money to pay the land taxes by then. Peter, take care of your Mamma and your sisters and brother. Remember how I showed you to use the rifle, keep an eye on the horses and chickens. That coyote was howling just west of the farm before I left. He would love to catch the chickens, and he would tear apart the coop. Matthew are you being good for your mamma, and hauling in wood? And little Emily, how is my sweet baby girl? Oh and I know that Pauline, you are helping mamma. You are always dreaming up something.*"

"*I have to get back to work now, my break is over. I want to get as much done as possible, so I can do the detail work,*" to get the extra money. I will write again next week, when I send home some money."

"Love, Papa"

Mamma danced around her little kitchen after she read the letter. "*Papa is working*" she cried. The children hadn't seen mamma this happy in quite awhile. It was good to hear mamma laugh and sing again.

Matthew asked "*Why are you crying, Mamma? Didn't you want Papa to work?*" Mamma started to laugh. "*Yes Dear. I want Papa to work. I have tears, because I am so happy.*" Matthew still didn't understand, but he sure liked that mamma was so happy.

Mamma said that after papa sent home some money, they could take a wagon ride into town, and pay on the land taxes. They seldom went into town as a family, now that papa was not home, except on Sundays to go to church. Mamma always made sure they got to church, and they would often visit a neighbor or have a family over for lunch. It seemed that almost all the township families did this. Sunday was a day of rest, and it kept all the neighbors up to date on the goings on. Sundays were also a day to help others, with building barns and houses, or helping a needy family in their fields. New families would come to settle in the township, and always needed help building a new house or barn. Mostly the men did the building, and the women would make a pot luck dinner. It was also a good way to meet the new neighbors.

In the winter, the visiting was kept to a minimum, because of bad weather, and the horses needed to get back into their barns for warmth. Once a month, in the winters especially, they would have a township meeting, usually on a Saturday, to keep everyone up to date on the township goings on, if anyone needed extra help, any one was having a baby, getting married, etc. Life here was sure a lot different than in the logging camp. People were a lot different, and seemed a lot friendlier. Mamma really loved it here.

They lived in Sawyer Township, in Waseca County. There were several county meetings, usually for farm meetings about crops, or auctions of farm animals and equipment. Most of these meetings were in the summer of fall of the year, when the weather was best for traveling. Sometimes, just the men would attend, but once in a while, the families would attend and have a huge picnic type meal, where each family would bring food to share. Women would share recipes and dress styles and patterns. The men would talk about farm things, new machinery, any upcoming auctions, and so forth. The townships held more meetings than the county did. It was easier to attend the local township meetings.

This year, a lot of the men were off looking for work. The prices of hay and corn were down, and there didn't seem to be very many new families moving into the area. With no one building new dwellings, the saw mills didn't need help. The tax men were getting tougher on families that didn't get their land taxes in on time. Papa had talked about taking a few acres and raising cattle. Everyone needs to eat, he would say. If the price of hay and corn don't go up, we can use it to feed our own animals, and not pay for it. Mamma didn't know if she liked that idea or not. *"What if the cows didn't breed well, or the calves didn't do well, what would they have to sell then and what would we do the first few years, when we were building up the herd?"* Papa would always have an answer, and said they would talk about it more, when he got back.

Mamma knew that papa was right, about the family needing to find more and better ways to make ends meet. She kept thinking that if papa was to work at the wood mill in town, then she would end up tending to the cattle, if that is what Ben decided to do. Matthew and Peter could help out too, and she was sure that Pauline would help, however she could. Then she thought about the size of a barn they would need for cattle.

How would they pay for lumber for a bigger barn? She imagined that Hans Miller would let papa work off the lumber at the wood mill. Mr. Miller owned the mill, and had let others work off their bills. They would still need quite a bit of money to buy the cattle. Ben didn't believe in loans, and even if he decided to give in this one time, they would have to deal with Mr. Smith at the bank.

So many things were rambling through mamma's mind; she laughed at herself, and thought she was acting like Pauline. 'It is no wonder that child day dreams' she thought; and with that she went back to her mending.

Peter and Matthew were hard on their clothes. Suzanne was always putting patches on the knees of their trousers. Matthew seldom got any hand-me-downs from Matthew, because they were all worn out before Peter grew out of them.

There was such an age difference between Matthew and Emily, that Emily got new clothes, not to mention the difference in genders. Suzanne had saved a few dresses from Pauline, and Emily had worn most of them out already. She crawled on some them, and wore out the front. Mamma saved them for play and when Emily went out in the fields with her. Now that Emily was walking, she wasn't quite so hard on her clothes.

Pauline saved some her dresses, as she got older. She put them in her trunk, in her room. She told mamma that maybe Emily could wear them when she got older, and that would save the family some money. She also had saved a few pairs of shoes that she had grown out of before she wore them out. Emily would have to get her own button hooks though, as Pauline's were all worn out.

Mamma saved some of papa's worn out overalls, to use as patch material on the boys' pants. Mamma was frugal, and didn't let too much go to waste. She had learned to save as much as possible, to reuse, when they lived in Illinois. Times seemed tough here in Minnesota, but when they remembered how little they had in Illinois, this was a much better life.

Suzanne was thinking all of this through, and came to the conclusion, that if Ben really wanted to raise cattle, she was sure they would manage. They would still have a few acres of hay and corn. Pauline was helping out as well. Soon

Peter would be old enough to do odd jobs, and make a little money as well.

The children were growing up so fast. Pauline was almost all grown up. She was nearly out of school, and would try for her teaching certificate, mamma hoped. Mamma had gotten her teaching certificate before her and Ben were married. She even taught school some, after they were married, but after Pauline came, she found it hard to teach. She had thought about going back to teaching after Matthew, but it never worked out, and then Emily came along. Mamma really had her hands full with four children, that she never gave it another thought.

Teaching was a good job for a single woman; it gave her an income and a little freedom and independence. If she were to teach in a different school district than where she was from, most townships would board her at the local boarding house. Other districts would board her as well, but deduct the rent from her pay. Mamma had been fortunate to teach in her own district, and was able to live at home, with Grandma and Grandpa Roberts.

CHAPTER THREE

◆

Pauline went over to Mrs. Kramer's right after school the next day. Pauline felt so bad that she had forgotten about working at Mrs. Kramer's the day before, she explained to her about the letter, and why she had missed work. Mrs. Kramer made sure that Pauline knew she understood, *"Why, of course Dear; your Mamma needed that letter, she has been expecting it. The Shoppe wasn't busy anyway, and I did all the mending in short order. You are always here on time so I knew something must have come up. Besides, Mrs. Davis told me about the letter from your Papa. I figured that is why you didn't show, dear."*

"Thank you Mrs. Kramer, for being so understanding, and I will understand if you take money out of my pay this week." Pauline said. *"What is there to do today? Are there any new orders for new clothes?"*

"No, dear, I will not take any money from your wages. You do such a fine job for me, and you are always so prompt." Pauline loved Mrs. Kramer.

"Well, Mr. Smith, you know the banker Smith? He brought in two suit coats to be altered. I took his measurements already. He would like the brown one done by Saturday noon. You know we have a 'Social" Saturday evening, don't you? He would like the black wool one done soon after. He always wears that one in the winter." Mrs. Kramer sometimes could ramble on, but Pauline loved to hear her stories. They were so interesting.

"Oh, I will do the brown coat right away. No I didn't know about the social. I'll be sure to tell Mamma. She could use some time away from the house and us children. I would be glad to watch the other children for mamma."

Pauline sat right down and started on Mr. Smith's coat. He was a snooty old man; Pauline thought and figured it was because he counted money all day, stuffed in that little office of his. Papa really never had anything nice to say about the Banker Smith. She supposed that people were really afraid of him, rather than disliking him, because he said if they got their loans or not.

Papa didn't believe in loans. It was *"cash on the barrel head or we don't need it"*, he would always say. She sure wished he would give in, especially when it came to the new shoes in the window of the mercantile. They had one inch heels, polished black leather with white ivory buttons up the sides. The ivory, Mr. Avery said, was straight from Africa, off elephant's tusks, and that is why the shoes cost so much. They were every teen girl's dream, and some women's too. They also came with a new matching button hook with ivory in the handle, and Pauline's old button hook was almost worn out. The shoes were four dollars. Two dollars and fifty cents more than the same style shoes she had gotten for the last few years. They were just plain black leather with simple black buttons up the front, nothing fancy at all. With four children to buy winter shoes for, Papa said he couldn't afford them, and *"They weren't practical"*.

Pauline dreamed of going to a social, wearing the new shoes and the new dress made from the little rose pattern. Oh if she had enough money, she thought she could buy the shoes and the material to make the dress; but Pauline knew she had to be practical too. The land taxes and food on the table came first. Besides, her brothers and sister would need new clothes and shoes, as they were growing up so fast.

It was hard to believe that baby Emily was two already. Soon, it seemed, she would be old enough to start school, Pauline thought. Mamma would be home alone all day, by herself. Even after papa came back from working in the factory, he might have to work away from the house during the daytime. Mamma was used to taking care of kids, Pauline thought, she might get lonely.

Then again, by the time Emily was that old, she might be able to start helping with the chores. She could dry dishes, and help carry little sticks of stove wood and kindling. Pauline knew that all that would be up to mamma and papa to decide. Now that Matthew was eight, she had hoped he could help Peter more, and Pauline could stay at Mrs. Kramer's a little longer in the evenings. Then she could make more money, and help out that way; and possibly save up enough to get the new shoes and the material for the dress. After all, she was almost sixteen. Mamma graduated school when she was sixteen, and she and papa were courting.

Pauline would lay awake at night, and wonder about growing up, getting married, and maybe having children of her own. But then, she would get sad, thinking about moving out of the house, away from mamma and papa, the boys and Emily too. Even though she and the boys sometimes would disagree, and mamma or papa would have to get after all of them, she loved her brothers.

They had moved away from Illinois, and all the other family that Pauline had ever known. Mamma's folks lived there, near them in Illinois. Papa's folks lived in Wisconsin, and came to visit a few times. Pauline had never lived in Wisconsin. She wondered if it was much different there, than Illinois, or where they lived now, in Minnesota. These two winters they had been in Minnesota, seemed to be much colder than Illinois, and there was a lot more snow. Pauline was glad that only lived a short way from town, especially in the wintertime.

In the summer, it wouldn't matter much. They would be not be in school for the summer, and the only time they had to go to town, was to get what they needed from the mercantile; and to go to church of course.

There was only one little church in town, and it was also used as the school during the week. That is the way it was in Illinois too, Pauline remembered. She wondered if all small towns were that way. Miss Frederick was the teacher this year, and Pauline thought her to be only a year or two older than herself.

Sometimes the boys in the class didn't want to listen to her. They would tease and tell her that her that she was young enough to be their sister. Pauline often thought that too, but was respectful to her, because she was their teacher. If the boys' fathers found out about them not listening to Miss Frederick, their papa's would take them out behind the woodsheds, and give them something to think about. Pauline had heard a few of the boys talk about such things, and after that they didn't misbehave in school.

Maybe if they had moved here a few years earlier, Miss Elizabeth Frederick and she might have been in school together, Pauline thought, instead of student-teacher, they might have been friends. She seemed to be very nice, and maybe after Pauline graduated, they would become friends.

Papa always wanted Pauline to try for her teachers' certificate. Miss Frederick might give her some pointers about the exams; Pauline was day dreaming again.

Pauline also wondered if Miss Frederick would attend the town social and if she already had a beau or not. She would never ask though, as that would be terribly rude. She rarely saw her teacher in town, except at school. Maybe she could ask mamma, but that might be rude as well, she would leave well enough alone. Mamma would scold her for her day dreaming again, and tell her to worry about her own affairs. Mamma was right, she thought. But still Pauline was curious.

There weren't a lot of children in this district, and sometimes there was a gap between ages and grades of the students. Pauline and two of her friends, Sarah and Emma, would graduate this year. She thought the Thompson twins were a year behind her, next was Matthew. She was not sure how many children were Matthews's age. There were more boys in school a few years ago, but most of them had to quit to help their pa's on their farms. Pauline knew a few of these boys her age around the township. It seemed that mostly girls actually graduated. Most girls then got teaching certificates. Pauline had only known one boy to graduate and go onto college. His pa owned the mercantile, and Pauline thought maybe they had a bit of money to send him. The nearest college that Pauline knew about was in Rochester.

Usually, the girls could take the teaching certificate tests at the local school, and the teacher could send them into the state. Pauline could study and take the exam about a month before she graduated, and then she should know by the start of the new school year, if she passed. Pauline was somewhat nervous about the whole situation. Not only had she seen what some of the boys did to Miss Frederick, but if Miss

Frederick stayed on in this district, then Pauline would have to go to another district. That would take her away from her family. She was not sure if she wanted to do that, but papa was always encouraging her to try.

She still had a few months to think it all over, and to really make up her mind. Maybe she could talk to Miss Frederick about it all, and mamma too. She need not fret over it now, she had her work at Mrs. Kramer's, her chores and her school work to worry about.

Anyway, she had a lot to think about, with papa coming home soon. Mamma would want to make a special meal for him, and Pauline could help; after all she was really learning to cook. Mamma had taught her the basic things as she was growing up, but now mamma was teaching her special recipes. Some of them had been handed down from generation to generation.

Pauline did not know of any recipe book, that any of these were written in, and thought that mamma must be very smart to remember all of them. Her grandmothers, great grandmothers, and so on, must have been very smart too. She hoped she would be able to memorize all these things as well.

CHAPTER FOUR

———— ✦ ————

Pauline had told mamma about the social, when she brought papa's letter home. Mamma hadn't heard about it either, and didn't know if she was up to going, with papa gone and all. She had so much to do around the house, not to mention looking after the other children.

Mamma had one Sunday dress, and she didn't think she wanted to wear it to a social gathering. She could not afford to buy more material to make another dress, besides the dance was too soon to even think of making a dress in time.

Mamma insisted that Pauline go to the social instead. She was too tired and would rather enjoy spending a quiet night at home, than go and *"listen to a bunch of hens, gossiping"*. Besides that, it was about time Pauline went to a dance. She would be sixteen in October, and graduate next

June. Pauline was shocked, but yet very glad. She really had wanted to go, and see for herself what went on at a social, but she wasn't sure what she would wear, and she knew it was impolite to ask mama if she could go instead of her.

Pauline never talked about any boys, except one young man that attended the school only a few times. Of course, with most of them Pauline's age helping at the family farms, the only place to meet them, was at church or a social. Mamma knew that there was a new family in the township, and thought Jackson was their family name. Mamma didn't want to rush Pauline into anything, but did think it was time to get acquainted with other people in the community.

Pauline had already met several families, as they brought their clothes to be altered or mended into Mrs. Kramer's store. Most of the children were younger than Peter, and she had seen them at school. Pauline was curious to know why so many people didn't do their own sewing, but then it may have been easier to let someone else do it. Besides, it gave her a job, and she had been able to see a lot of the new families in town.

Mamma hoped Pauline would find herself a nice wealthy business man, and not marry a dirt farmer like she had. Oh Mamma dearly loved Papa, but life was hard. Papa didn't have much of an education, but he was a hard worker, and wasn't afraid to work, to put food on the table. He was a good provider, mamma would always say. Papa would just smile, and go on doing whatever he had been doing. Pauline thought he rather liked the compliment once in awhile, although she thought him not to be a 'proud' man.

Mamma helped Pauline dress in mama's own best dress for the social. It was light mint green, tight around the bodice and the shirt flowing to the floor. Mamma had trimmed the collar with a piece of lace that she had tatted herself. The sleeves were ballooned at the top and narrow at the wrist. There were ten buttons up the back. Mamma had covered them with the dress material to match. Pauline had a hoop underskirt that held the hem just above her shoes. "*Oh, thank goodness I just got my winter shoes*" Pauline thought. They were still kind of shiny and had only a few scuffs.

"*Thank you mamma, for letting me wear your dress. I promise not to ruin it. Do you think it is too low cut? Oh mamma, I am a little scared to go all by myself. How will I know what to do?*"

"*Shush child, you are rambling on. You will do just fine. You will have friends there, and you know most of the folks from the township.*"

Mamma made ribbons from dress material. She helped Pauline put her reddish-brown hair up in a bun, and wound the ribbons through and around it. She left the tails of the ribbons hang down her back. With her hair in a bun, Pauline looked older than she was, especially since she always wore it down or tucked into a bonnet. She thought she looked prissy with her hair up. After all, she was only 15 and a farm girl.

Soon, it was 6:30, and time to go into town. Mamma had arranged for Mr. Kramer to pick up Pauline and bring her home again. Pauline was nervous, since she had never been to such a gathering alone before, and to go alone. But mamma assured her that there would be other girls her age there. Pauline had friends from school, and they might be able to sit and talk, and maybe "gossip" like the "hens" mamma laughed about.

There was that new family in the township and Pauline noticed they had a boy near her age. She wondered if he would be at the social. He had only been at the school a few times, as he had to help on their farm. She wondered if he had to help with the hay and the corn too or the animals, or if his papa had to go find work. She was daydreaming about all of this as Peter yelled *"Mr. Kramer's coming"*.

"*SSSH!*" Mamma hushed him. "*They can hear you in the next county, boy.*"

"*Hello sir*" Mamma said to him. "*Pauline will be right out. Thank you for seeing after her. I am just too tired to go, and I have to stay with the baby. The boys should not be left alone either.*"

"*No problem, Ma'am. I will pick up Selma* (that was Mrs. Kramer's first name, although Pauline had seldom heard anyone call her that) *on my way back into town. She was not ready when I left to get Miss Pauline.*"

"*Miss Pauline*" Pauline thought. No one had ever called her that before. It sounded kind of, well, grown up. She would be sixteen soon. "*Hmmmm*", Pauline thought about it, "*Miss Pauline. I rather like that*".

Pauline walked out of the house, and Mr. Kramer gasped for a breath of air. He had never seen Pauline wearing such a grown up dress before. It was very revealing in the cleavage area. Mr. Kramer's face turned a shade of red. After all, he was a married man, and shouldn't be noticing these things of other women. He hurried to get back to pick up Selma.

Pauline's dress was one that mamma had made several years ago for herself, and wore to church and socials. Papa had rather liked the dress, and had often said so. It was not long after mamma made the dress and wore it a few times, that baby Emily had come along.

Mrs. Kramer was all ready to go, when they returned. She was waiting on their porch, a shawl around her shoulders, and a new purse in hand. Mrs. Kramer had made the new dress herself. She had told Pauline it was for Sunday best this winter, but when they picked her up, she said she could hardly wait to wear it, and thought the social might be a good time to try it out.

Mr. Kramer had on his usual brown suit. Of course Mrs. Kramer had made that too, some time back. She made all their clothes, with her dress shop and all, she said that she would never buy clothes from the catalog in the mercantile, not when she can make them, and make them her way. She would talk about the "new" styles from out East and Europe, and how they were getting so bold, and it was just not becoming of a lady to have so much skin showing. Pauline kind of wondered what Mrs. Kramer would think of her dress, as the front cut so low.

CHAPTER FIVE

◆

Pauline walked into the town hall, following Mr. and Mrs. Kramer. Mrs. Kramer had on the beautiful dress she had made, which was a royal blue chiffon, with a very flowing skirt. Since Mrs. Kramer was a stout woman, it wasn't made tight in the bodice, but it still made her look beautiful. She had trimmed it with light blue lace imported from France. It was very expensive too, thought Pauline. For she had seen the price of it when the shipment came in; seventy-five cents a yard.

Mrs. Kramer added a white shawl and matching bonnet, just as she said she would, and she had ordered a pair of shoes, just like the ones that Pauline had wanted. Pauline hadn't known that Mrs. Kramer had ordered herself a pair, and she was a bit jealous.

Pauline squinted her eyes from coming in from the dusk, into the bright lamp light. She was looking for her friends and thought she might see that new boy as well. Before her eyes had a chance to focus, a hand touched her arm. *"Can I have a dance on your dance card?"* The voice came from a tall thin outline of a person she thought she recognized, but she didn't recognize the voice.

"Why, I haven't even gotten my dance card yet. I have just arrived."

"Well, can I get us each a cup of punch, while you get your card?" unfamiliar voice seemed to crack a bit.

Pauline felt a little embarrassed. Already a suitor for a dance. She hadn't even gotten all the way into the hall. She went to the table where the dance cards were neatly arranged; she looked for her name among the cards. Someone had taken a lot of time to make the cards. They were heart shaped, a light pink, with neatly painted wild flowers on them, and of course the girls' names were printed neatly on them too. Inside were six lines, for men's names for the dances. There was a red ribbon tied neatly around for their wrists, and there was a little pocket for the little pencil that was put inside.

Pauline found her card, and when she went to turn around, she almost bumped into the young man behind her holding two cups of punch. "*It's him*," she thought, the new boy she had seen at school. She was surprised that he had been looking for her, and she felt her cheeks getting hot from blushing. She hoped they weren't as red as they felt.

"*For you, Miss*" as he held out a cup towards her.

"*Thank you. . . . I don't even know your name.*" She said in a sheepish voice.

"*Oh, I'm sorry. We just moved here. Jackson, Homer Jackson. We just moved here*", he repeated himself. "*I've seen you in town a couple of times, and at school too. But I haven't been able to go to school very much, with the farm and all. I have to help out my pop.*"

"*Glad to meet you Mr. Jackson.*"

"*Can I have a dance on your dance card, then, Miss Mayfield? It is Mayfield, isn't it?*"

"*Yes, how did you know?*"

"*I inquired with the post mistress, after you left there the other day.*"

"*Oh! I guess you can have a dance on my card*" she shyly muttered. "*Please let me finish my punch first, Mr. Jackson.*"

"*Call me Homer, please. I am a farm boy, and 'Mr.' just doesn't suit me.*"

"*Yes, ok Homer. And please call me Pauline. Are you going to be attending school after the fall harvest? Yes, I have seen you a few times there also.*" Pauline thought about what she had said, and thought it awkward, as she was still blushing. She was babbling she thought of herself. He must think she is a little bold.

"*No Miss, I mean Pauline. I quit school to help my Pop run his new farm. I tried to attend, but with the chores, I could not keep up on my school work, and pop said I need to be a man, and help out.*"

The music started and it was a Waltz. All the other couples started to dance, as though they had been at a social before. Pauline felt a little awkward, but yet she was excited about being there.

"Shall I fill your card?" Homer inquired.

"Fill it 'ALL' in?" Pauline asked, getting a little more embarrassed. She had just actually met Homer. How could she let him fill her card? Men only did that to a ladies card, if they were courting her or they were already engaged.

"Well,. . ." his voice trailed off. *"I meant to fill in a line, um and I thought since we were close in age, maybe we could. . . . . ."* He didn't finish. He was embarrassed as well and his face turned red.

"This dance, Homer" she said. *"Here's my card."*

Homer quickly wrote his name on her dance card., and they began to dance. Homer was a good dancer and he never stepped on her feet once. He was a perfect gentleman.

After the first dance, Pauline sat down near her girlfriends. They talked and giggled some, as none of them had ever been at a social either. They all were a bit shy when asked to dance. Pauline waited for another boy to ask her to dance, but no one came over to ask Pauline. So eventually Homer asked her for another dance, and so that was how the evening went on. Homer filled her dance card, plus they danced couple of dances that weren't on her card.

Pauline didn't know some of the dances, but her and Homer did their best to keep up with everyone else. When they would fall out of step, they would just laugh at each other. It was a grand time. Sarah and Emma danced with several of the young men. The three girls would often try to stay near each other, while they danced, and would give silly glances at each other. It was a time to just have fun, and they did.

Soon it was time to go home. The evening had gone by so quickly. Pauline had a wonderful time, talking with her friends, but especially dancing with Homer. What would mamma think when she saw her dance card. Pauline felt her cheeks getting warm again.

The ride home in Mr. and Mrs. Kramer's carriage was cool in the evening breezes and the cold dew that had already rested on the ground. You could see the dew sparkle on the ground under the almost full moon. It was a beautiful night, Pauline thought, and Pauline was still warm from all the excitement, and the dancing, but she was also flushed thinking about telling mamma all about the social. The stars were twinkling overhead. It was a beautiful night, and all Pauline could think about, was dancing with Homer Jackson. It seemed like a dream to her, and he seemed to be a real gentleman.

Pauline thanked Mr. and Mrs. Kramer for the ride into town and back home again and then made her way into the house. Mamma was waiting up for her, but the children were fast asleep. Pauline was grateful for that, as Peter could tease Pauline a little too much sometimes. He had teased her before she left for the dance, that her dress was too low cut, and he thought it to be gross. He had not really noticed girls, except to tease them with toads and worms. He thought all girls seemed to be a bit prissy.

Pauline was hoping that when Peter found about her dancing with Homer all evening, he wouldn't make a big deal of it at school on Monday. It may have been the town social, and most of her friends already knew, she wasn't ready for him and the boys at school to tease her about it, and he would.

Matthew was a bit young to pick up on some of the things Peter teased about; Pauline was happy about that. In her heart, she knew he would soon learn. Emily, being the baby, the boys might look out for her, rather than tease her about such things. Time would only tell, she thought.

CHAPTER SIX

———◆———

Papa sent home at least five dollars a week, depending on how much detail work he managed to get done. He kept one dollar and fifty for himself each week, for his room, meals, and his train rides. After a few weeks he came home for the weekend, just like his letter had said. He didn't send money that week; he brought it with him instead. He was thinner now, but his family was so happy to see him, it didn't matter. Mamma especially, but she did comment to him, that he should be eating more.

The mail system seemed so slow, that even though papa didn't send a letter that week, one came from a week before. Papa thought that was rather funny, and wondered how he might send his letters to coincide with his visits home. It was hard to calculate, since sometimes the mail came right through, and other times, it took weeks. So papa decided to keep doing it the way he had been, and try to keep the money coming in for mamma.

"I've been waiting for a home cooked meal for a long time." Papa said. *"Restaurant food is ok, but it is never as good as my Suza's cooking, and I see Pauline is learning as well. Plus I just miss the company of my family, eating alone is no fun."*

Mamma had made a pork roast from a pig she bought from a neighbor. She had used some of the money Papa had sent home. There was also fresh bread, boiled potatoes, corn from the field, and of course one of mamma's wonderful apple pie.

"Suza" Papa spoke in his stern voice. *"That money is for our land taxes, but this is a wonderful meal. No one can cook like my Suza"* and his voice was much quieter now. Mamma blushed.

* * * * *

Land taxes, the government didn't make it easy to own the land. Two dollars an acre and fifteen dollars for the house. They didn't tax the barn or the out-house. Papa thought the taxes to be rather high, but where else could he get twenty acres of good farm land? It would be their farm, their land, and they would not have to move again; unless, of course, they chose too. So paying the taxes and farming the land was worth the effort, he would say, but only after complaining about the land taxes. Papa never imagined that he would he would have to go find work elsewhere, and hated being away his family. He would apologize to Suzanne and the children, for the extra work it was putting on them. He also did not like leaving them alone on the homestead.

There hadn't been trouble with Indians in many years; and there hadn't been any other trouble lately, like rustlers or 'squatters' trying to illegally gain ownership of homesteads. A few years back, there were several of these squatters, which would try to intimidate a homestead family, get them to move, and take over their farms. Troubles with the Indians were virtually all over with.

The government had stepped in, and laid down the laws on these situations. Even still, papa worried about leaving his family alone. Papa taught Peter how to use the rifle, and said he would be the man of the house until he returned. Peter was to defend the family against any threats, human or animal.

There was always the threat of bears, wolves, coyotes and the like. The chickens always seemed to be the most vulnerable. Papa had to chase away several wolves and coyotes since they had set up their homestead. Peter was instructed to try and chase away any such intruders, and to shoot to kill at the last resort. After all, they are all *"God's creatures"* papa would say. Papa and mamma liked the natural setting they had there on the homestead.

Pauline could not imagine mamma and papa wanting to ever move again. This was such a quaint house. The *"little orchard by the creek"*, the creek and all trees made it so beautiful, plus they had a garden; which they did not have room for in Illinois. Mamma planted lots of vegetables and some fruit in their garden. She canned all she could in the fall, and they ate 'fresh' vegetables and fruit in the winter. A lot went in the cellar. How could anyone ever want to move, and leave all this? She knew she was happy here, and wasn't sure she would ever want to leave herself.

Soon, before they knew it, the weekend was gone. They had talked about what had been happening at home; and what papa was doing in Rochester. How they missed papa, and he missed them. Everyone wanted papa to hurry home for good. Papa was glad to get to church on Sunday morning. Reverend Black was a good preacher, and papa missed his sermons. There were so many churches in Rochester; it was hard for papa to choose one that the thought had the closest doctrines as their little church in Sawyer Township. The church in town was called "Sawyer Community Church".

Papa would be leaving on the evening train, back to Rochester, back to work at the factory; and it would be back to the fields for Mamma too. Mamma would have to take papa out to the train station. It was about three miles west of town, but it was closer than that to their homestead. Pauline would stay home and watch the children. Mamma was gone about four hours, and was ready to put the horses in the barn. She didn't like taking the wagon at night, but said it was worth it to have papa home. Papa had gotten a ride home from the train station from a neighbor. Mamma wasn't sure when he would be able to come home exactly, and papa had surprised her.

Now papa figured that he should be able to come about every three weeks, but it would all depend on orders at the factory. He would try to send word to mamma when he could come home next. Papa said he would also try to get a ride home from the train station, so mamma would only have to go one time when papa got a trip home. There was always someone at the station, it seemed, and he could most likely always hitch a ride. He didn't tell mamma, that if he couldn't hitch a ride, he would have to walk home, but mamma knew.

Pauline would go to school with the other children on Monday morning and back to work at Mrs. Kramer's after school. Emily would just play like she always does; after all, she was the baby.

Peter asked mamma, again, if he could quit school, like that Jackson boy, and help on the farm. Mamma seemed to get a little angry, and told him that she had already made that decision. He was to stay in school. Mamma didn't agree with Mr. and Mrs. Jackson, and said that "*the Jackson boy*" should have stayed in school. "*He will end up being a farmer, just like his papa and your papa*", mamma said. Pauline wanted to know what was so wrong with that. She was proud of papa.

Matthew piped up, and said that if Peter got to stay home, he wanted to also. Mamma got a little riled up with that, and scolded the boys. "*I want my children to grow up and make something of themselves. You need schooling, and no one is quitting school in this family, if I have anything to say about it.*"

The children were glad they had riled mamma *AFTER* papa had gone back to Rochester. Papa might have taken them out behind the barn, for sassing their mamma and getting her upset. They were also hoping that mamma would forget about it before papa's next trip home. They knew better, but they were somewhat confused; how could they go to school, and help mamma with all the chores. The boys knew they should not ask mamma about quitting school again. Next time, she would tell papa, and they would get taken out behind the barn for sure.

Mamma may have gotten riled, but in her heart she knew that the boys meant well, and only wanted to help out. She figured the chores they did after school, was plenty enough work for them to do. Peter hauled water in from the creek, and Matthew still was hauling in stove wood and Pauline made sure the beds were made, before school. The rest of the chores would be done after school. Homework could be done by lamplight after the chores were done. If there was still daylight after the chores were finished, the boys were allowed to go fishing.

On Saturdays during the summer and early fall, after all the chores were done, the children were allowed to go to their friends to play, or have a friend over. Pauline often went and helped Sarah or Emma with their sewing, and sometimes one or both of them came to the Mayfield's to help Pauline. Mamma would often make sugar cookies and lemonade for the children as a treat. In the winter months, it was often too hard for the children to get around as much. If their was too much snow, school would be cancelled, but on days when the snow wasn't so deep, occasionally a neighbor would pick up several children on the way into town, with their own children. Mamma and papa had even made several of those trips. The parents would kind of rotate, picking up the children for school. When it was warm, or there was not so much snow, the children walked to school. The older children always looked after the younger ones.

The school was a one room building, with children's school desks that also served as pews during church, a desk for the teacher, and a black board. There was a wood stove in the back right corner of the building, with a wood box next to it. The children took turns bringing in wood, when it was cold enough that they needed a fire in the stove.

There were four windows on each side of the building, and one on the front, next to the front door. There was a door on the right side of the back wall, which had a path that led to the out-house. Just inside the back door, on the side wall, there was a small stand with a pitcher and bowl, for washing hands. The inside walls, were plain wood planking, which was cut from 'Miller's Mill'.

On the left side of the back wall, stood the pulpit, which Reverend Black used on Sundays. The teacher's desk would be shoved back against the wall, to make room for the pulpit. The black board was behind the teacher's desk. Reverend Black's wife, Rose, made a curtain that was drawn over the black board for church services. She also made matching curtains for the nine windows. The curtains were very basic, plain light green with matching tie backs. The curtains could be closed if the sun shone in a certain window, and made it hard for people to see.

Along the inside of the front wall, there were hooks for coats. A shelf ran across, over the hooks, for lunch pails and such. On Sundays, the shelf also served as a place for the gentlemen to put their hats during the services.

The township voted on the building, and it would serve as a school and a church. The wood floor would creek when even the smallest child walked across the room, but they were all grateful for the wood floor, as they had heard other townships had dirt floors in their schools.

There was an outside stair case that led to the attic. The attic was used to store school books in the summer and extra desks. The attic could also be used for plays, dances and other functions. The women would sometimes assemble in the upstairs room of the school, and make quilts and other items for the county fair.

The outside of the school, was white washed every summer. There was a bell in the belfry, which served as a school bell and a church bell. It could also be used to alert the community of any emergencies.

Reverend Black was happy to see papa, and the other men that had gone to look for work, in church on the Sunday's they were home, and said so. He also told papa and the other men, he understood that they had to look for work, and that he and Rose would check on their families. Papa was grateful for that, and told mamma that it would help him concentrate on his job at the factory; although he would still worry some. Mamma understood, as she worried about papa while he was gone.

CHAPTER SEVEN

---- ✦ ----

The next time Papa came home, he brought something with him; it was a musical jewelry box, for Pauline's sixteenth birthday. He would miss the actual day, but he didn't forget her birthday. It was beautiful, and when she opened it, a dancer would whirl around and the box would play a waltz. The box was wood, painted blue, with little dainty white flowers that looked like miniature roses, painted along the sides; some of the flowers were carved in as well. The box reminded her of the night of the social, and papa had remembered how excited she was to tell him about that night. Pauline's birthday was not til the following week and papa would have to be back in Rochester by then.

Mamma and Papa decided to celebrate Pauline's birthday the weekend when papa was home. Pauline didn't care that it wasn't her actual "birth" day, but that papa was there, and the rest of her family. Family, that is what makes the difference, she figured.

At Pauline's birthday party, she was allowed to invite her two best girl friends; and of course Peter, Matthew, Emily and Mamma were there, but the best thing was, that papa was home. Mamma made one of her apple pies, as they couldn't afford much, and there was fried chicken, biscuits and gravy, and homemade lemonade. Ben and Suzanne also bought Pauline a new shoe button hook. Peter and Matthew made her homemade birthday cards, with promises to help her with her chores, although Pauline didn't expect them to hold up the promises. It was a grand party, Pauline thought; she just wished homer had been invited, too.

Homer and Pauline had gone on several picnics and buggy rides together, as they were starting to be more than just friends. Also, the time they spent together helped pass the time in between Papa's visits. Sometimes they would take Pauline's brothers and sister with them, to give mamma some time alone, or sometimes they would just take one of the children. Mamma even attended some of the picnics, and once Homer's folks attended as well.

When mamma and Homer's parents all came, it was the first time they had all formally met. Pauline wished that

Papa could have been there; then Homer could ask him if he could 'officially' court Pauline. The two of them had talked about it, and agreed they would like that very much, with all their parents consent.

Homer had two brothers: William and Zachariah, and a sister Eileen. They would often take them on the picnics and rides as well. Eileen was fourteen; she and Pauline often talked at lunchtime at school, even before she met Homer. Pauline never knew Eileen had an older brother until the night of the social. She had never put two and two together, because Homer seldom had attended school. Eileen really had never mentioned Homer to Pauline that she could remember. She knew William and Zachariah from school. They were very smart boys, but they harassed the girls also.

Soon there was snow on the ground. Buggy rides gave way to sleigh rides. Mamma hoped papa would be home for good soon. He had been home for several visits, but not as often as he had wanted to; so mamma could hardly wait to have him home to stay. Mamma sold the hay for twenty five dollars, and the corn went for a tidy sum as well. Mamma had saved fifty five dollars of the money Papa had sent home. Mamma was carefully counting the money. She kept in it an old snuff can of Papa's. She had fifteen dollars of the hay money left. Pauline contributed twenty dollars. All together they had ninety dollars. It was enough to pay the land taxes, and may even have a nice Christmas, especially if Papa got home in time. The land taxes would be Sixty five dollars for the year. Before any thing could be bought for Christmas, mamma and papa would make sure everyone had good winter shoes and coats, and that there was food in the house. Papa also wanted to replace the milk cow.

Homer continued to come around a little more often now, since the farm chores were less in the winter months. Pauline was glad she had met Homer, and he was always pleasant and polite. He never tried to kiss her, either. Although, she might not object too much if he did try. She was sure that Homer felt the same way, as they had talked about it, but mamma had told her stories of young couples courting, and then breaking it off for different reasons.

Mamma allowed Pauline to invite Homer for supper once in awhile, and Pauline was also invited to the Jackson home. She really liked Mr. and Mrs. Jackson. They were always very kind to her, and she and Eileen were quickly becoming best of friends. It was nice to have someone close to her own age to talk to about girl things. The boys just didn't understand girl things and Pauline didn't want to share everything with them.

Pauline, Sarah, Emma and Eileen would often have sewing parties, or help each other with school work. Eileen was a couple years younger than the other girls, but she fit right in. She was also very smart, and was trying to learn two grades at one time, so she could graduate early. So the other girls often tested her on learning material she would need to know to pass on to the next grades. Eileen's goal was to graduate with Pauline, Emma and Sarah. Miss Frederick said it was possible, if she studied very hard and doubled up on her school work.

All four girls thought it would be great if they could graduate together. They could have a party or a picnic, or maybe even a dance. They all helped each other to memorize what they needed to and learn all their assignments. Since the four of them started working together on the school work, their grades had all improved greatly. Miss Frederick was very impressed. She was so impressed, that she went to the school board, and asked if it would be ok to let a few students' pair up, to help each other learn easier. Also, the older students could sort of tutor the younger ones, while Miss Frederick was helping other students or grading papers and such. After the school board saw how much improved the four girls grades had become, they agreed.

Pauline thought it was a good way to learn to possibly become a teacher herself, besides that it was fun. The girls would all laugh and giggle, and make games of the school work, to make it easier to learn. Pauline had to schedule her time with the other three girls, around her work at Mrs. Kramer's.

* * * * *

One night at Mrs. Kramer's, Pauline had an idea. She asked Mrs. Kramer if she could use some of her money she would earn, to buy material and make clothes for her family for Christmas. It would be a complete surprise to them, and they would never think to look there, especially the boys. They liked to snoop for their presents. Mrs. Kramer said that was a grand idea, but she would have to get all the stores work done before working on her own things.

Pauline made a new dress jacket for mamma, a new shirt for papa, and for the boys she made each a pair of trousers. For Emily, she made two new dresses, as she was growing so fast. Pauline made one more item, that she kept a real secret. She made a plaid wool shirt, for Homer.

Pauline hoped that mamma and papa wouldn't think that she was too bold, or that Homer would be offended. She really liked Homer and wanted to make him a gift as well.

This all took time, and it was a good thing that Pauline had started early enough, or else she would have never gotten them all done by Christmas. She stayed up late a few evenings to do her school work, so she could work at Mrs. Kramer's a little longer.

Peter and Matthew were asking mamma to do odd jobs to make a little money, so they could buy the family something for Christmas. They also wanted to know if they could ask the neighbors, or at the mill or mercantile, if they could do a few odd jobs. Mamma and papa had decided that if they got all their chores and school word done, they could.

Ben and Suzanne were surprised at how fast the children were growing up. That they were thinking of other family members, and not just themselves. They had tried to instill family values, and it seemed to be working. They were very proud of their kids.

There were little secrets all over the house, and the town for that matter. People were busy looking at this or that, and making deals. Even at school, the children were making homemade cards to give to their families for the holidays. At church, the children were practicing a play, for the Christmas holiday.

One year Emily got to be Baby Jesus, in the church play, but now she was too old and wouldn't lay still. All the children got to play a part, even if it was only to be an angel or a Wiseman. Miss Frederick talked to the school board, and they all agreed, that the church play could also double for the school play. So they started practicing earlier in the year, before Thanksgiving, as it would also be graded as a school activity.

Miss Frederick was so good at directing and managing it all. She made it fun as well as educational. She took the story of Baby Jesus being born in Bethlehem straight from the book of Luke. She wrote out the parts, for Joseph and Mary and all the other characters. Peter, being the oldest boy, would have to play the part of Joseph.

Miss Frederick said the part of Mary would have to be voted on, as well as other parts. She wanted to know, if anyone on the community had a young child or baby that could play the part of Baby Jesus. She also wanted to know if anyone could help in making costumes. One of the families in the township had a young child, and they agreed to let their baby be "Baby Jesus" in the play. Mrs. Kramer said she could help with some of the costumes, but she could not afford to donate all the material. Other parents had old clothes that could be used as well. They made due with all that was given, donated and made.

Emma got the most votes to be Mary. Sarah was to be the Angel Gabriel, who told Mary that she would "bring forth a son, and shalt call his name JESUS". Matthew was one of the Wiseman, along with the Thompson twins, Isaiah and Samuel. Eileen would narrate the play, as she had the best voice, the class decided. She was also to recite most of Luke chapter two, the Christmas story. Pauline was to be one of the shepherds, and other children were the donkeys and other animals.

Pauline was thankful that she didn't get voted to be one of the main players, as she wanted to get her presents all sewed at Mrs. Kramer's. It would be a grand play, and she was excited to be in it and help, but also wanted to surprise her family with the gifts she was making.

The play was to be shown on December 23rd, in the Church/School building. It would start at 4:00 p.m., with a pot luck dinner afterwards, for all to celebrate Christmas together. Every family, that attended, would bring a casserole or dessert, and they would just have a fun time. It was a time to celebrate all that they had, and to get to know any newcomers to the township.

The children could play games after the dinner as well. Since it was winter, there weren't any crops to be attended to, and most of the livestock could be taken care of before or after the festivities. Of course the parents love to see their children perform in the play. It was a wonderful play, the students performed it the best as they possibly could. There were a few mistakes, but no one mentioned that they had noticed them.

CHAPTER EIGHT

———————— ✦ ————————

Thanksgiving came and went in the Mayfield home. Without Papa home, it wasn't much of a celebration. He had to have his Thanksgiving meal in a cold restaurant in Rochester, by himself. Mamma made her and the children a baked chicken dinner, with boiled potatoes, and biscuits. Oh, yes, she made one of her wonderful apple pies. They had picked the last of the apples before the frost, and stored them in cellar under the kitchen floor. Pauline made stuffing out of an old loaf of mamma's bread. She used gravy from the chicken to flavor it. Mamma even said that it wasn't too bad either, and that Pauline was learning quickly.

On December 15th, a Friday night, there was to be a Christmas Dance at the town hall. It was an annual event. There was generally a good turn out, with the boys done with chores early now; it was a time to see "Who was sweet on whom". Of course, married couples came too. Homer asked Pauline to the dance.

Since the Christmas Dance was a yearly event, Miss Frederick didn't give the students homework for the weekend, and said they would forego the play practice for that evening. It was a break for everyone; even Miss Frederick, because she would not have so many papers to grade on Monday morning. She could use the time to help students with school work, or help them memorize their parts for the play.

Pauline wore the same dress to the dance that she wore to the Social in September. Mamma removed the lace collar. It made the dress more revealing, Pauline thought. She blushed at the thought, but she was sixteen now, and soon she would graduate. She was becoming a real lady. It also, made the dress look different, and maybe no one would notice it was the same dress. Mamma or Pauline could not afford to make or buy a new dress. Pauline added different hair combs, and did her hair differently as well.

Homer arrived in his sleigh. He was usually exactly on time, but this time he was early, and Pauline was not quite ready. It was a cold evening. Homer had put hot coals in a baking pot, with a lid, on the floor between where their feet would go. He also brought several blankets, to keep them warm on the way into town and back; and he could use them to cover the horses while they were at the dance. He had put sleigh bells on the horse's harnesses and it was rather neat to hear them coming. He said he wanted it to be a special evening for the both of them.

Pauline hurried to finish getting ready. As she went out to the sleigh, she didn't think she was late, and wondered if she had misunderstood the time Homer said he would be there. *"Good Bye Mamma"*, she said as Homer helped her into the sleigh.

"I'm sorry I'm early. I didn't mean to rush you, but I have something to ask you."

"Oh my goodness, I didn't think I was late. When I heard the sleigh bells, I hurried. Homer, what is it? Is there something wrong?" She had remembered what mamma had once said about couples breaking up, and was afraid that Homer didn't want to see her anymore. She was even starting to have tears welling up in her eyes, and got a lump in her throat. What would she say or do, if Homer didn't want to see her anymore, she thought.

Homer was busy driving the team, and didn't even notice the tears, or that Pauline was getting nervous. He was also busy thinking how to say what he needed to, without sounding foolish, or having Pauline taking it the wrong way and be offended.

"I have been saving my money, for a down payment, to buy my own farm. I am seventeen now. I have enough money now. I plan on going to the assayer's office Monday, to apply for a twenty acre homestead. I have a little extra money to start building a house and a barn. Pop said he would give me one of his milk cows, two butcher piglets, and some chickens, to help get me started. And. . . ."

Pauline interrupted, *"What does this have to do with me?"* She just knew then that he was going to tell her he had another girl, or wanted time alone. She tried not to let the tears fall, or let Homer hear her voice quiver.

"Pauline, please let me finish" Homer's voice cracked. *"I also had enough money to buy this."* He pulled out a small box from his pocket. *"Open it"*, he said as he handed it to her.

"What's this?" Pauline inquired. Now she was very confused.

"Go on, open it. I ordered it special, for you."

As Pauline opened the small black box, Homer started to speak. "*Pauline would you. . . . .*" his voice cracked.

"*Oh, it's beautiful!*" Pauline quickly interrupted Homer. It was a blue sapphire stone in a beautiful ring setting. "*But what is this for. It's past my birthday, and Christmas is yet over a week away.*"

"*Would you marry me?*" he said very quickly, and then he tried to kiss her.

Pauline backed away in shock. "*Marry you?*" She didn't know what to say or do. She never expected this, not now, not yet.

"*Yes, marry me Pauline. Please be my wife. Please say yes.*"

"*Why, Homer Jackson*" she yelled at him. He thought she may jump right out of that sleigh, and say 'NO'.

"Have *you talked to my Papa, Homer? Or Mamma?*"

"*No, not yet. I wanted to talk to you first, Pauline. We've been courtin' for a few months, now, and I L. . . L . . .*" his voice cracked again. "*I love you Pauline*". After a pause, he said again, "*I want you to be my wife.*"

"*It's all so sudden. I mean, I really like you. We have had so much fun together. But I guess I never thought we were ready for an engagement.*"

"*I thought you might show your new ring off, at the dance tonight. THE DANCE!! We better get there before we're late.*" With that, Homer snapped the reins and the horses started to trot. They had been sitting nearer Pauline's house than to town, all the while.

The snow wasn't too deep. It was really beautiful, sparkling against the moonlit sky. '*It is so romantic*' Pauline thought. She didn't know how to answer, or if she should before talking to mamma, or before Homer talked to papa. So many thoughts were running through her mind. What would her friends say? What would Mamma and Papa say? Oh my goodness, she thought, am I really old enough for this? She felt like the words were spinning around inside her head. She did have feelings for Homer, but was she ready for all of this?

As they rode towards town, she kept thinking about what Homer had just said to her. She remembered the stories, of how young mamma was when her and papa got engaged and married. She was sixteen, and would graduate soon. Somehow it was all starting to make sense to her, she was old enough.

As they were on their way to the Christmas Dance, Pauline spoke up. *"Let's go down by the creek, just outside of town. Can we? The water isn't frozen, yet, is it?"* she added.

"No, I don't think it is frozen yet. We can go see."

They soon were sitting in the sleigh, next to the creek. The water was softly rippling by. The frogs were gone for the winter. It was all quiet, except for the water and the soft breezes blowing by. The reflection of the moon danced on the water as the breezes caused the water to ripple, and it was so beautiful. Her mind was full of thoughts and questions.

"Homer, can I see the ring again?" She had given the box back, as she wasn't sure of her emotions, or what she should do with it. She thought she loved him, and she thought she was growing up. If he loved her and she loved him, what would be wrong with an engagement, she thought.

"Oh, yes, here it is", he said as he pulled it out of his coat pocket.

"*It is so beautiful. Yes, Homer, I will marry you. I guess you had better put the ring on my finger, if I'm going to be your wife*", and she held out her left hand. She felt little butterflies in her stomach.

Homer took the ring out if its little box, and managed to put it on her ring finger. A perfect fit, and he had only guessed at the size. She had such dainty hands; he didn't think the ring had to be very big. After Homer slipped the ring on her finger, he started to kiss her.

Pauline had never been kissed by a boy before. Well, except for Papa and her brothers, and that just wasn't the same. It was a weird feeling, she thought, as their lips touched. She had a tingling feeling and was a little light headed. All of a sudden, she began to giggle like a school girl.

"*Me*", she giggled. "*Getting married. Oh when? Homer, when should we get married?*"

Homer started to laugh too. "*Well, I think we should get to the dance first. We can discuss that later. I have to talk to your Pop first, and we'll have lots of time to plan a wedding.*"

"*Oh, yes. The dance*", her voice sounded as though she was floating.

At the dance, Pauline only showed the ring to her two best friends, Sarah and Emma. They thought it was a beautiful ring. It was a single band with etching around the outside, and a blue sapphire stone, which was her birthstone. Pauline didn't want the news to get back to Mamma or Papa, before she had a chance to tell Mamma, and Homer could talk to Papa. Sarah and Emma promised not to say a thing to anyone. It would be their secret.

Pauline and Homer danced every dance together. But this time, they really seemed to float across the dance floor. They had sparkles in they're eyes; and everyone noticed that they truly looked 'in love'.

On the sleigh ride home, Pauline thought, 'What am I going to tell Mamma?' The ride was so light and airy. They laughed and talked all the way to her house.

"Oh, Homer, I've had a wonderful evening. And I . . . ", she stopped. *". . Love . . . . . you too"* she added. Yes, she really loved him. She really did! Homer kissed her again.

"Will I see you tomorrow?"

"I don't know. I have a lot to do. Planning and getting ready to buy "our" land."

"Ok", she said. *"It will give me time to talk to Mamma anyway. Papa should be home next weekend for good. Are you going to talk to him then?"* Homer helped her out of the sleigh.

"Yes, I plan to. I love you, Pauline" And with that he hopped into the sleigh and was gone. Pauline danced into the house. Her feet felt like she was walking on clouds. Her heart was pounding though.

"Mamma, guess what?" she half yelled into the house.

Mamma told her *"Hush, you're going to wake the youngin's"* Mamma was sitting in her rocker, knitting. The other children were already in bed for a few hours. *"What is it, dear? How was the dance? Is everything all right?"*

"Mamma look", as she held out her hand for Mamma to see her ring.

Mamma's eyes grew wide. *"Oh, it's beautiful, Pauline."*

"Oh yes Mamma, it is beautiful. Homer promises to take care of me. Forever!"

"Does this mean what I think it means, child?"

"Yes, *Homer asked me to marry him. He wants to talk to Papa the next weekend he is home. Oh mamma, do you think I should have waited and not said yes so soon. What do you think mamma?"*

"Pauline dear, Papa and I knew this day would come. We have seen how you look at that Jackson boy, and how he looks at you. You will graduate school soon, and are working more and more at Mrs. Kramer's. You are so grown up, and I married your Papa at your age. I do not see where there is a problem, or that papa would object. But we will see this weekend when he gets home."

CHAPTER NINE

———————— ✦ ————————

Papa came home on Thursday, the week before Christmas. It was two days earlier than Mamma anticipated. She was happy to see him, but he looked so tired. It was obvious; he had lost a lot of weight.

"It was a long train ride home, Suza. I am so tired. I have missed you and the children so much, and I am glad to be home again"

"Are you home for good, Ben?" Mamma asked, in a voice that was full of hope. Pauline had rarely heard mamma use papa's real name, which was actually Benjamin.

"Yes Suza, I am. I never want to leave you again. The money was good, and we needed it. I love you, Suza, and I

missed you. And the children." His voice trailed off. They hugged and kissed.

"*Oh, I love you too, Benjamin Mayfield. And I missed you so much. I hope we never have to endure another hardship like this again.*" Mamma kissed him again. Mamma and Papa were so happy and the children could see the spark back in their eyes.

* * * * *

Mamma was a small framed woman, and she had kept her figure, even after all the babies. She had a tired but youthful face. After all, she was only thirty three. She was eighteen, when Pauline was born. She and Papa had been married almost two years then. They had courted a year before they were married.

Mamma always wore conservative dresses. She wore an apron when she was working, and of course her bonnet when she was outside. Sometimes the bonnet was around her neck, when she was working in the fields. Mamma had long red hair that she put up every day, and brushed out every night. Papa loved her hair. He always said it looked like the flames of a fire dancing in the sun light. She always took her bonnet off and hung it on the nail, by her shawl, next to the front door, when she was coming indoors.

Mamma had a saying, which she got from her Mamma, 'Everything in its place, and a place for everything'. Mamma kept a very neat house. She made sure the days dishes were done every night, even if the children were to do them. She swept too, after the dishes were done and put away. She washed the lamp globes once a week. Usually on Sunday nights, to make sure of good reading light for school work. She was very thoughtful that way. Of course the children helped with all of the chores.

Papa was also a thin man, but very muscular. He kept himself in very good shape. That's what attracted Mamma to him, some nineteen years ago. He had a thin moustache, and otherwise, was clean shaven. His hair was a golden brown, and a little bit wavy. It was always clean cut. Mamma kept it cut short, using her sewing sheers, as they could not afford to go to the barber. He stood, Pauline figured, about six feet tall. Mamma was about six inches shorter than Papa. They made a very cute couple.

Mamma thought Ben to be the most handsome man she had ever seen. She and her family had moved to Waseca, Minnesota, when she was a very little girl. She and Benjamin

Mayfield had gone to school together and they hadn't always liked each other, they fought as school children. Suzanne thought him to be an immature brat in school; until they were teens, that is, then love bloomed.

Papa and Mamma had moved to Illinois, soon after they were married, so papa could work in the logging camps. A lot of families were moving to the logging camps, as jobs were numerous. Mamma's family had also moved to Illinois. Papa's family moved to Wisconsin. Pauline remembered hearing the stories, of there not being any work, so families were moving away. Everyone was looking for good employment. The logging camp served its purpose. Mamma and Papa moved back to Minnesota to homestead the farm, they wanted land to own themselves, and not pay rent.

Papa was tired of moving around, and just wanted to stay home, and be a family man, run the farm and maybe do a few odd jobs in the county. He could always help build new homes for new homesteaders, or barns and other outbuildings. There were always roofs to be repaired, fences to mended, papa was sure he could find work. This had just been a hard year to save the money for the land taxes. There were more and more families moving into the area on new homesteads, so he was sure there would be more jobs next year.

Chapter Ten

✦

Monday morning, Homer went to the assayers' office, as planned. He wanted to get land near town, but far enough out to be quaint. There were two parcels left, fitting that description. The one Homer picked, was almost half way between his parents farm, and the Mayfield's. He figured it would be close enough, so Pauline wouldn't get lonesome.

He went to put his markers out, with the surveyor, and it was then he found a perfect spot for a house. It was into a hill, with oaks and pines all around. It would be shady and cool in the summers, and out of the winds in the winters. He wanted to talk to Pauline, before he started building the house. But he could start on the barn and fences right away, but he was sure this was where they would want their house. It was the perfect spot, overlooking the creek and the rolling hills. The front of the house would look to the South, with the North wall set into the hill. That would help out with the heat of the summer and cold of the winter months, as well. Then he thought, it could also have shelves for pots, pans and other dishes Pauline might want to put in there.

Homer stood looking at the area, and decided in his head, that he could dig out and build a root cellar into the hill, and that could be attached to the kitchen area. Pauline would never have to climb up and down a ladder, to get into the cellar, she would be able to walk right into it, and get what she wanted or needed. He smiled to himself, as he thought that was a great idea. He just hoped Pauline would think so as well.

He went back into town, to order lumber for the barn, then he went directly out to the Mayfield Farm. He wanted to show Pauline the land right away. He was so proud and excited and needed to share this moment with her and to ask her advice on the location of the house, if she would agree with his ideas or not.

This was Homers first true love, and would be his first time leaving home. He hoped Mr. Mayfield would get home soon. He wanted to get that talk over with. He was very nervous about talking to him. What if Mr. Mayfield said

'NO'? His stomach was in knots over it. After all, he had already bought the ring, land and lumber.

The children were home now, as school was let out for Christmas break. Homer was really hoping that they would not want to go with him and Pauline. He wanted to show the land to her alone.

"*Pauline*", homer shouted, as he got close to the house. "*Can you come with me? I have something I want to show you.*"

"*Homer, settle down. I can not understand a word you are saying. You're talking so fast.*"

Homer repeated himself, only slower this time, and not shouting. "*Can you come with me? I want to show you something?*"

"*Can I Mamma?*"

Mamma nodded and smiled. She remembered young love. Homer and Pauline went to see 'their' new property. Homer had no idea that Ben was home early, but thanked Mrs. Mayfield for letting Pauline go with him.

They went straight to the homestead Homer had just acquired. Homer showed Pauline where he thought a house would go nicely among the trees up against the hill, and where the barn could go. He wanted to know what she thought about it. He told her he had chosen that parcel, for the location, so she could still be near her family. Pauline cried tears of joy, and thanked him for being so thoughtful, and then she hugged and kissed him. She thought it to be perfect.

"Homer, my papa is home. He was in the barn when you arrived. Mamma has talked to him, and he is waiting for you to come and talk to him. Mamma wouldn't tell me what papa said. He wants to talk to you, mamma said, and she could not go against him. Oh Homer, I am so scared. I do love you. I am afraid that papa will not give his permission for me to marry you." With that she began to cry, and said *"You have gotten this land, and ordered the lumber already. What will you do, if papa says no?"*

"Oh my dear Pauline, I love you too. I will talk to your papa. I am scared too, but if he knows how much I love you, I do not see why he would say 'no'. Besides, I am old enough to be moving out on my own. I will need a homestead either way, but I really want to spend my life with you. I want to be

as happy as both our folks seem to be." He gently kissed her and she kissed him back.

They talked for a long time, and they noticed it was getting dark. Pauline said she had better be getting home. Papa would surely be unhappy if he kept her out late. Homer agreed, and he took her home.

* * * * *

Homer came right over, the following Saturday. He was nervous, but Pauline was pacing the floor. Mamma still would not let on, what she and papa had talked about, what papa had said. She wondered if Grampa and Grammy did this to mamma and papa when papa came to talk to them. She had butterflies in her stomach, she thought were big enough to carry her away.

"*C'mon Dear, let's go out and check on the chickens. While the men folk talk*" Mamma said. "*We need to get in the eggs anyway. Maybe we should check on the horses and the cow.*"

"*Mamma, what do you think papa will say? I am afraid mamma*", Pauline started to cry.

Linda Habeck

The other children were outside playing in the newly fallen snow, they were taking turns sliding down the hill, and pushing Emily down a small snow bank. It was great fun. Plus it kept them out of the house while Homer and papa talked.

Back in the house, Ben poured himself a cup of coffee. *"Want some?"* He asked homer.

"No sir."

"What's up son?" Ben asked, knowing full well what he wanted. Mamma had already spoken to him, but he wanted Homer to ask for his daughters hand.

"Well, Sir, I. . . I"

"Speak up son. I won't bite ya."

"Can. . . I. . have your daughter's. . . hand in . . marriage? Mr. Mayfield. . . Sir?" Homer blurted out in an uneven voice, that even seemed to crack.

"Have you thought about this? From what I understand, you only met my daughter in September."

"*Yes Sir, I have. I. . love her, Sir. I have land now. Near by, so I wouldn't be taking her far. You can come see her anytime you'd like, sir.*"

Ben started laughing. He told Suza he was going to let Pauline marry Homer. He just wanted Homer to be man enough to ask him. He couldn't control the laughter any longer.

Homer couldn't see the humor in this. "*Sir, I'm serious.*"

"*I know you are, son. But you remind me of myself, when I asked Suza's father for her hand. I was just as nervous.*"

"*Yes, Sir. I can understand that. I do love your daughter sir, and I really want t...*"

"*Quit calling me 'Sir'. I'm a poor dirt farmer, and if you're going to be my son-in-law, you had better get used to calling me 'Papa'.*"

"*You mean it, Si - I mean Papa?*"

"*Yes, Homer. But I want Pauline to take her teachers exam, and graduate first. I think she would make a wonderful teacher, don't you? And you had better take care of my baby girl. Have you talked about a wedding date yet?"*

"No, not yet. I wanted to talk to you first."

"Well you had better go talk to my daughter. She may want to agree on a date, don't you think? Thank you for coming to me, and for being a man. That has made all the difference in my decision."

* * * * *

Homer ran out of the house, almost forgetting to shut the door. Ben was still chuckling to himself. Mamma went in, and left Pauline and Homer to talk.

"Oh Suza, it was just like when I asked your papa for your hand in marriage. I think that young man was shivering in his boots. Just like I was, remember? And your papa made me ask him, and just sat there, and let me sweat. I couldn't do that to that poor boy, I started laughing so hard."

"Ben, our baby girl has grown up. She is gonna get married and move away. Now I know what my mamma felt. I am happy, yet so sad."

"*It's ok Suza, that young man has gotten himself a homestead near ours, so she will not be far away. He has already ordered the lumber for the house. He has a head on his shoulders, and I am not worried about our Pauline.*"

CHAPTER ELEVEN

❖

Christmas was just two days away. Ben and Suza had been out walking on their modest homestead, and found a beautiful little pine tree for the children to decorate for Christmas. There was just a light fluffy layer of snow, and mamma told papa, how it really made it seem like the Christmas season. The tree only stood about three feet tall and was just big enough to sit on Papa's smoking stand. Papa didn't smoke, but the stand had been his fathers. Papa used his hatchet to cut down the small tree. He brought a rope with them, to drag back a tree, but this one was light enough, that papa threw it up over his shoulder and held on with one hand. Papa held mamma's hand with his free hand, as they slowly walked home, enjoying this peaceful time together. Anyone that would see them at this moment would know that they were truly in love.

After they returned home, mamma made popcorn for the tree; and some to eat, too. Pauline, Peter and Matthew cut stars, bells, trees, angels, other designs out of old newspapers. The children would string the popcorn on thread, to make garland for the little tree. They would also use a flour and water paste to starch the newspaper cut outs, so they would retain their shapes on the little tree. Papa had gotten the newspapers from the paper office, for ten cents a bundle. They were old papers that no one had bought, and the newspaper office saved some of them for just these kinds of things. Mamma kept a tin on top of the cupboards with candle holders and candles, made especially for the Christmas trees. Papa always put the candle holders on the tree with the tiny clips attached to them, and then he carefully set the candles into the holders. The candles would only be lit on Christmas Eve and Christmas Day for an hour or so each; any longer than that and the tree might start on fire.

The tree would be absolutely beautiful with the candles lit, Pauline thought. Emily was old enough to really like the tree and all its decorations. Keeping her away from the tree tended to be the problem, as she wanted to touch the 'pretties'.

Just as they started making the decorations, there was a knock at the door. 'Who could that be', papa thought, as they weren't expecting company, so he got up to answer the door. The door hinges squeaked against the cold temperatures outside. As he opened the door Pauline could see that it was Homer.

"Can I see Pauline, Mr. Mayfield, I mean Papa, please?"

"Sure, come in out of the cold, son."

"I bought you something for Christmas, Pauline." He handed her a small package wrapped in newspaper and a string, which he had tied into a bow. *"Go on; open it, please."* he encouraged her.

Pauline was embarrassed, and her cheeks showed a pink hue. She hadn't thought to have Homer's present ready yet. Her hands shook a little as she tried to tear the newspaper wrapping.

"Oh, it's beautiful" she delighted as she opened it. It was a small mantle clock that stood about 7 or 8 inches tall. It was made of cherry wood, and had a rounded top and the clock itself was set into the wood. The glass face was hinged, so you could open it to wind it with the little 'key' that came with it. When the hour hand reached the hour mark, it would play a little tune, a waltz. It reminded her of the dances she

had danced with Homer, and she smiled a sweet smile. All of sudden the embarrassment was gone, and butterflies were fluttering inside of her. Were these signs of young love?

"I thought you would like it on 'our' mantle, when I get our house built."

"Oh yes. I love it Homer. Thank you. But I haven't gotten a chance to get your present ready. And it's not quite Christmas."

"I will have you soon enough as my wife, and that's enough for me. Just a moment, I have to get something else from my sleigh." Homer hurried outside. He came back in carrying a big wooden box.

"This is for all of the entire family" he said. *"Go on, please open it, Sir"*

"I thought I asked you to call me 'Papa'?" With that, Papa grabbed a hammer from his wooded box of tools, and opened the crate. There was a large turkey, yams, homemade stuffing, and homemade bread; everything a family needed to make a perfect Christmas dinner.

Mamma began to cry. "*We can't accept all this, Homer. We have nothing to give you and your family in return*", she said. "*Please, ma'am. My mom made the bread and stuffing for you; Pop went out on our homestead to get the turkey especially for you, the yams are out of mom's garden. Mom, pop and I talked about this, and we wanted to do this. It is a token of our appreciation, as well as for Christmas. For letting Pauline and I become engaged and just for being our friends.*"

"*Well, then you are to join us for Christmas dinner; and your family too. That will be our present to you and your family.*" Papa announced.

"I *will tell Mom and Pop you have asked them to dinner. As for me, I'd be honored to. What time shall I be here for dinner?*"

"*Tomorrow at three. Dinner is at three, and we are not asking you and your family to dinner, we are . . . .* "Mamma smiled, "*demanding that you and your family join us. 'We' would be honored to have you all here. We usually eat a big dinner on Christmas Eve, and go to church on Christmas Day. Will you be joining us for church, as well?*"

"I will be here at three, and I am sure my folks will be too. Yes, I would rather enjoy joining you for church. Thank you, but I must be going now." Homer turned to walk out, and then he turned around. *"Pauline, I love you my dear. I shall see you tomorrow"* and he kissed her cheek quickly.

After Homer left, Pauline asked mamma if they could talk for a few minutes. *"Mamma, what can I get Homer's present wrapped in? Can we go to town? Do we have enough time? Can we. . . ".*

Mamma interrupted her, *"Yes, Dear. We will go into town in the morning. I will put the turkey in to bake, and Papa shall drive us in. Won't you, Ben?"*

"Yes, Suza. What ever you want."

"There now child, can you relax the rest of the evening and quit that fidgeting? We shall make sure you have the gift for homer wrapped nicely. We have enough to do in this little house, before tomorrow comes" mamma said with sassy smile. She knew Pauline was too anxious to relax, but was hoping to get her mind off of it, long enough to help with the last minute chores that needed to be done.

* * * * *

Dinner was served at three O'clock on Christmas Eve, as planned. Homer, his parents, sister and his two brothers were right on time. Pauline and Suzanne worked on the meal almost all morning and into the early afternoon. They had finished cleaning the little house, as well. There hadn't been very much to do, just sweep the floor, and make sure that everything was in its place. Of course, they found time to go into town to get wrap for Homer's shirt. Pauline wasn't going to let anyone forget about that.

Pauline and the boys set their modest table. Pauline folded the linen napkins and placed one on each plate. Fresh milk was in the pitcher, and mamma made fresh coffee. Mamma even got out a small dish of sugar. Lard and sugar on the fresh bread would be a treat for the Mayfield family. The boys could hardly wait until dinnertime.

The Christmas tree was placed neatly on papa's smoking table, in the corner of the living room area of the big room. The smell of fresh pine made the house seem more inviting, and all the tree trimmings were placed perfectly, Pauline thought. It was truly a season to celebrate. The candles would be lit for dinner, and the little tree would be beautiful.

Mamma and papa's rocking chairs were pushed up to the table for extra seats, the flour barrel was brought over and one of the boys sat on that. Mamma and Elizabeth decided to eat after the men and the children ate, as there just was not enough room for both families to sit at the table. The two smaller boys shared a chair, and at first, were scooting one another off the chair, until Mr. Jackson gave Zachariah the 'look'; then they sat all perfectly still for the rest of the meal. Eileen and Pauline sat on the floor in front of the Christmas tree. They chatted about their gifts they had made their family members, school, and other 'girl talk'. Pauline giggled like a school girl, and for a few moments forgot about almost being grown up and being engaged.

Seth and papa talked about farming, their homesteads, and other manly things. They laughed, and joked as well. The meal was as excellent as it smelled. Everyone seemed pleased and enjoyed themselves.

After dinner, Pauline gave Homer his present. She had made him the flannel shirt. He loved it. Also, the Mayfield's gave the Jackson's two of Mamma's wonderful apple pies to take home; in addition to the pies she had made for dinner. The pies weren't near as much as they had received from the Jackson's, but it was all they could afford, along with sharing the Christmas Eve dinner. It was a wonderful dinner, and a perfect day. The sun was shining brightly outside, even if the temperatures were below freezing, which made the snow sparkle. It was absolutely beautiful, Pauline thought to herself.

The next morning, before church, the Mayfield family exchanged Christmas presents amongst themselves. Papa had gotten Mamma a new Sunday dress. It was cotton; blue, to match her eyes, he said, with hand embroidered roses around the collar. Mamma was so surprised. She wasn't sure when he had time to order it as it was surely one of Mrs. Kramer's creations, and how he knew what size to get, but then again, that didn't matter. It was a beautiful dress, and she couldn't wait to wear it to church.

Mamma got Papa a new brown leather hat. His was worn from years of wear. Papa always wore a hat when he went to town, and said it would be a great day to wear his new hat to church. Peter got a wooden car papa made, and an orange; Matthew got a wooden train engine, and his orange; and Emily got a new rag doll and of course her orange, but she wasn't about to let loose of her old doll. Pauline got the shoes that she had wanted; the polished leather ones, with white ivory buttons up the sides; and the matching button hook with ivory in the handle, and her orange. She was so surprised, and very happy. She would save this button hook, until her other new one wore out. It was a wonderful Christmas for every one in the Mayfield home. They may not have had a lot of money, but they were blessed and rich with love. The family was very close to one another, and Pauline thought that made all the difference. Her and her brothers argued at times, but she loved them and knew they loved her.

Baby Emily was too small to be involved with any of the tiffs the other children may have had, but she still managed to get into things, and make a mess. She seemed to get away with more than the other children had at that age, but Pauline figured that was because she was so much younger than them.

CHAPTER TWELVE

———— ✦ ————

It was hard to work on the barn in the winter, in the cold and snow, but Homer worked on it every chance he got. He tried to get out to it everyday, even if for just an hour or two. He really wanted to get it finished, so he could start on the house and cellar, as soon as the weather warmed.

He and Pauline had been discussing how the house should be. Pauline wanted a separate living room and kitchen. Mamma's and Papa's was one large room. Homer was worried about the cost. He did have a job at the lumber mill, but it didn't pay all that much. He worked on his own lumber, which saved them a lot money. He had gotten the job shortly after placing his first order. They needed a strong young man to handle large orders. He was allowed to work on his own lumber before and after his shift and during his breaks, or if it was a slow day.

Pauline worked on some of their curtains at Mrs. Kramer's Shoppe, after her work was done. Homer had ordered a large window for the living room. She could at least get those curtains done, since she had the size of the window. Her and Homer picked out a white cotton material, and Pauline was embroidering flowers along the bottoms of them. She mostly embroidered red roses, green leaves and stems, but she added a few other flowers here and there for additional colors, such as purple violets, yellow black-eyed-susans and other wildflowers. She drew the handmade patterns for the embroidered areas on a piece of paper, and then traced them onto the fabric. Mamma had taught her how to make the patterns as she was growing up, and how to trace the patterns on the material. Mamma also taught her to embroider. Mamma had made all the family's linens, and had embroidered on most of them. Pauline thought them all to be pretty, and had wanted to learn how, so mamma had taught her several years ago. Pauline was glad that she had taken the time to learn.

Homer and Pauline decided on one large room for now. They could add on in a few years, if they wanted to. It would also be warmer in the winter with one large room. Pauline decided that she could place the furniture in several different ways, with one big room. They could also add partial walls between the two areas later on, and still have an open area for air circulation. That would suit both Homer and Pauline, making it look to be two rooms and still be easy to keep warm. They decided they could wait on that until much later, after the house was finished, and they were caught up at the lumber mill.

Homer asked Peter to help him, after school, to work on the house. Sometimes Matthew would come and hold lumber while Homer sawed. Homer's brothers, William, 13 and Zachariah, 8, came and helped as well. They all enjoyed helping and it gave the boys a chance to become better friends. They knew each other from school, but now played together more. Homer never talked down to any of them, but rather would praise their work and treated them as young men. They took pride in their work and tried hard to do everything the right way. They all appreciated being treated in an adult fashion, rather than like kids.

Homer's mom helped work on the curtains for other windows in the house, in her spare time, as well. She had some old quilts, she had made years ago, that she offered to Pauline and Homer, for their new home. Homer and Pauline were happy to have them, and appreciated them. They were prized as heirlooms to them and would be happy to use them.

* * * * *

As spring neared, Homer and Pauline wanted to throw a picnic to thank their families, for all the help they had given them; as the barn was nearly completed. They would go down by the creek on Homer and Pauline's land, find a flat spot that had enough room for the kids to play, and close to the creek so they could go swimming as well. That same creek, Tallgrass Prairie Creek, wound through the Mayfield Farm, around town, and over through the Jackson Homestead. The creek was full of small fish, toads and turtles. There were small falls, over little bunches of rocks here and there, which made a beautiful rippling noise.

Pauline planned a large meal with fried chicken, homemade biscuits, homemade canned peaches, and apple pie for dessert. Pauline hoped the apple pie would turn out half as good as her mammas. As the children played together, the six adults and Eileen would talk all afternoon.

Elizabeth asked Pauline, "*Do you have a wedding dress picked out, yet?*"

"No, *Ma'am. I haven't had time to think about it yet. With helping getting things ready for the house, working at Mrs. Kramer's, and keeping up with my school work.*"

"Well, Child. I would be honored to have you wear the dress I was married in. My mother made it for me."

Suzanne started to cry. She knew her and Ben could not afford another expense, and could not afford to buy a dress or the material to make one either.

"Have you kids set a date yet?" Seth asked.

"Well, we were thinking about the second weekend after Pauline's graduation. She graduates on May 24th." Homer replied. *"If that doesn't interfere with any of your plans. We wanted to ask all of you, 'our parents', what you thought of that weekend. Planting season is over and harvest is a ways away."*

Elizabeth and Suzanne talked to each other about it, as well as Ben and Seth. Eileen, Pauline and Homer just looked at each other puzzled. What would their parents think about their plans? They knew they would have the final say in the date they wanted to get married, but they still wanted their parents' blessings.

After several minutes of all four 'parents' chatting amongst themselves, they all turned and looked at the couple, and said almost all at once; *"That sounds like a wonderful idea."*

Seth also stated; *"We appreciate your concern with the farms and homesteads, but it is ultimately your decision. It is your day, and it should when and where you both want it"*

After that said, Seth turned to his wife; *"Well, Betsy"* That's what Seth called Elizabeth. *"Shall we go home, and get our chores done?"*

"Yes, Dear. It is getting late isn't it?"

Mr. and Mrs. Mayfield left shortly after, went home and relaxed. They were happy that the Jackson's' were helping the couple out as much as they could, as it took quite a burden off of them. They wanted to do as much as possible, but they just didn't have the finances to do much.

On the wagon ride home, Seth and Elizabeth also talked about the day, and agreed that they and the Mayfield's were doing as much as they could for their children. They were very happy for Homer and Pauline. It seemed that they were made for each other, and got along wonderfully. They also really liked and enjoyed the company of the Mayfield's. Pauline had also befriended Eileen, and encouraged her to study harder and try to graduate early. Eileen needed her friendship as well.

* * * * *

What Ben and Suzanne did not know, was that Mrs. Elizabeth Jackson was very well to do. Elizabeth did not flaunt it, and the Jackson's did not dress or act in such a manner. Homer had to work at the saw mill to 'work' for his lumber. Ben and Suzanne wanted their children to know what it was to work for a living, and not think themselves to be better than others.

Suzanne grew up in a well to do home, and her Father flaunted it. She never had many friends, as they all thought her to be snooty as well. Even though she had all the finer things growing up, it was not a happy childhood.

Suzanne loved her parents, and knew that they did the best they knew how, in raising their family. She wanted her children to respect their belongings, and others as well. When Ben and Suzanne got married, they talked about her wealth, and both decided that they would live modestly, and would work on a homestead. They would not receive any of her inheritance until her parents passed on.

The Jackson children did not know the truth in their mother's inheritance. When her father passed away, she became well to-do.

CHAPTER THIRTEEN

✦

May was here before they knew it, with all the graduation and wedding plans. Pauline graduated second in her class, of five; only being outdone by the preacher's son, Teddy Black. In addition to Pauline and Teddy, there was Sarah Johnson, Emma O'Keefe and Eileen Jackson in the Graduating Class of 1868. It was a small ceremony, on a Sunday afternoon; a picnic followed, then a dance. There was a grand turnout. Again, Homer and Pauline danced all the dances together.

After graduation, it was finally time to make serious plans for the wedding. Pauline, with the help of Mamma and Elizabeth, sent letters to all the grandparents, Aunts, Uncles and Cousins right after the news of the engagement, and the upcoming marriage of Pauline and Homer on June 7th, 1868. Of course the entire town was invited. Reverend Black would officiate.

The wedding would be held in the town church, with the reception following in the town hall, and of course there was a dance.

Elizabeth helped Pauline and Suzanne with the alterations to the dress. It was beautiful white chiffon, with lace and intricate beading covering the bodice and the flowing skirt. It had a four foot train. It was very elaborate, with the material originally coming from Paris, France. Elizabeth and Seth were married in Boston, Massachusetts. She was from a very wealthy banker family, and they had a very expensive and formal wedding.

The wedding dress had tight fitting arms, and a high neck collar, with lace from the collar to the very low cut revealing cleavage area. The bodice was tight to accent (then Elizabeth's) Pauline's beautiful figure. It also had silk covered buttons down the back; there must have been fifty of them. The under skirts had four hoops to make the skirt really full and flowing. The train could be buttoned up, in the back, with matching buttons, for dancing. Pauline also would wear her Christmas shoes, as they made a wonderful accent to the dress. Pauline was going to be a beautiful bride.

The veil had long since been lost, with the Jackson's move from Boston out west to the homestead land. Pauline would wear wild flowers in her hair. Mamma made a wreath of them, put Pauline's hair up, and would have flowers around the bun as well.

* * * * *

Pauline carried a bouquet of wild flowers to match her hair. Emily was the flower girl. She threw wild flower petals, all the way up the isle of the church. She was pretty as can be, with her pastel green dress. She was almost three now. Homer's brother, Zach, was the ring bearer. He looked like a real gentleman, carrying the ring pillow up the isle. Peter Mayfield and William Jackson were the groomsmen. They wore their Sunday suits. They each had a wild flower in their lapel. Two of Pauline's friends from school, Sarah Johnson and Emma O'Keefe, were her bridesmaids. They each wore a pastel Sunday dress. They also carried a bouquet of wild flowers. Although their bouquets were smaller than Pauline's. Homer's sister, Eileen, walked behind Pauline, to keep the train of the dress straight. She wore her Sunday dress as well, and held a small bouquet of flowers.

Homer wore his best Sunday suit. It was black, and he wore a freshly made white dress shirt that Mrs. Kramer made in her shoppe; and a tie Elizabeth had imported from

England. She decided that he should look as handsome, as Pauline was beautiful.

It was a beautiful Sunday and the sun was shining brightly. The church was full to overflowing. Homer was as nervous as a cat under a rocking chair. Yet, he could hardly wait to see Pauline. She was beautiful any day, but today, she would be as beautiful as he could ever imagine.

The organ began to play. Papa walked Pauline down the isle, after Emily, Zach, Peter and Sarah, and William and Emma. The whole church stood. They all were in awe, of her beauty. Mamma and Elizabeth were crying. Seth was smiling from ear to ear. They were all so happy for the two of them.

As they reached the alter, Homer embraced Pauline's arm with his. Papa gave his daughter away, and sat next to Mamma. Homer and Pauline gazed into each others eyes, as they said their vows. Always to love one another. To be faithful. To cherish one another. And to live out their lives together. It was a wedding to be remembered for a long time. There wasn't a sound to be heard through out the ceremony, except the minister, Pauline and Homer; everyone was as quiet as church mice.

As the Reverend Black said, "You may now kiss your bride", Homer and Pauline embraced in a long passionate kiss and all the guests stood and applauded.

At the town hall, the newly married "Jackson's" danced the first dance, and everyone ate. There was baked chicken, ham, potato salad, deviled eggs, punch and a beautifully decorated cake. It seemed as though this night would never end. Homer and Pauline were so happy.

Pauline and Homer spent their wedding night in a hotel room in town, as 'their' house was not yet finished. It was just the local hotel, nothing too fancy, but it did not matter to them. They were too much in love to care.

CHAPTER FOURTEEN

After spending the night in the motel, Pauline and Homer, went to the "Mayfield's" to stay until their house is finished. Pauline was helping with their house in her spare time, to help finish it as soon as possible. They were both anxious to start life in their own home.

It took almost a month to finish the house. Homer and Pauline packed all their things in their wagon, and took them "home". Their first night in *THEIR* home. It would almost be like their wedding night all over again. It was so exciting, to be alone, in their own home.

It took Homer and Pauline, only a short time to put their household things in their proper places. They had a milk cow, a few chickens, and a pig to take care of as well. Seth had given Homer and Pauline a pregnant sow, that they would be able to have more pigs and have a fresh supply of meat.

They also got a rooster, and decided to start raising a few chickens for cooking as well. Homer had already tilled up a spot for their garden. With the creek near by, they would have water easily available. Pauline thought it was a lot like being at her parents' home, but was glad it was her home with Homer. They were so much in love.

In the kitchen Homer had built in a sink area, with a work counter, for Pauline to prepare meals on. They had a wood stove that double as a cook stove. It had an oven big enough for a roaster pan. It also had a small compartment just big enough to bake bread. Pauline could bake meals as well as bake bread. Homer had also built in a warming chamber over the fire place. If Homer was late for a meal, she could put a plate in the compartment to stay warm until he came home.

The wood stove was against a wall, that separated the kitchen area from the bedroom area. Pauline made a curtain, at the dress Shoppe, for the bedroom doorway. Homer and she picked out the material together for the curtain. They ended up agreeing on the same material for all the window curtains, and bedding. The material was not only pretty, it was a quality material that would last a long time. Mrs. Kramer had also said that it was a good material.

Homer had made a small table and two chairs. They bought two rocking chairs from a local man that made furniture. Pauline made chair pads for all the chairs. Pauline had her trunk from her childhood for her clothes. Homer had a small chest of drawers from his.

Under the sink, there were cupboards for pots and pans, and other kitchen necessities. Homer built an upper cupboard for plates, cups and all the dishes. Pauline had suggested a cellar and a pantry, as Homer was building the house; since he was finished with the outer walls, Homer cut a doorway in the kitchen, and added a small room, for a walk-in pantry. There was also a trap door in the pantry floor that went to the root cellar.

Pauline has so excited and happy about her pantry and cellar. Now she knew she would be able to put up fruits and vegetables and store them for the future as well as the winter months. She was very anxious to start the garden. She was hoping it wasn't too late to start the garden.

* * * * *

Homer, with the help of his father and brothers, had built the modest barn before the house was built. It housed the cow, pig and the four horses. Two horses were for the wagon. The other two were work horses for pulling the plow and other machinery. Homer had bought hay and put in the 2nd story of the barn. He also had a space for grain, other animal feed and seeds for the land. Homer had taken care, to put in small window openings in the second story, to let out heat and moisture, to keep the feed, grain and all the other items fresh. He had heard from other men that their grain and feed items had either molded, or combusted and the barn burned. Homer was trying to keep that from happening.

In the window openings, he put fencing to keep birds and animals out, but also to make sure nothing was accidentally pushed out the openings. The window cutouts were on hinges and Homer made them like shutters, so that they could be opened when needed, or shut in bad weather. Pauline thought Homer was such a smart man. It was one of the things made her love him so much.

Pauline had helped Homer with the fence around the corral. Homer dug the holes to set the posts in, and Pauline helped with the rails. Homer made the fence four rails high. His Pa's fence only had three rails, and the smaller pigs were always getting away. Homer thought, that by making his fence with four rails and the lowest rail lower to the ground, he might keep that from happening.

He and Pauline also put chicken wire around on the lower two rails to the ground. They hoped that this would also help in keeping smaller animals inside the corral, and unwanted animals out. The cost was more than they originally anticipated on spending, but thought it was worth the expense.

Homer built the chicken coop himself, also before the house was built. He made the coop with two rows of shelves, hoping that they could raise several chickens. Pauline was hoping she could store eggs in the cellar, and sell extra ones when they needed the money. Homer put a chicken wire room on the door side of the coop, with a gate. This hopefully, would keep out anything that would threaten the chickens' lives. Also, they could feed the chickens without them getting loose as well.

* * * * *

Pauline and Homer's first night in their home was a quiet one. They fed all the animals together, and then Pauline made supper. She made stew, made of beef from Homer's parents. They had bought vegetables in town, as they didn't have their garden yet. Pauline also made a bread to go with their supper.

Pauline had hung her night gown on a nail in the bedroom when they unloaded the wagon earlier. So when it was bedtime, she folded her dress and under skirt carefully laid them in her trunk. She carefully put her shoes next to the trunk. She washed out her stockings and hung them in the kitchen for the next day. She and Homer went to bed for the first time in their home.

They both were so tired, they fell right to sleep. Tomorrow they would have more work to do. Pauline would start to plant the garden, and Homer would work in the fields. Homer had planted the fields earlier in the year. They had field corn, wheat and hay. Pauline would plant eating corn in the garden. She hoped it would grow big enough to eat in the growing season they had left.

CHAPTER FIFTEEN

✦

It was September, and near Pauline's seventeenth birthday, when Pauline woke up one morning and was so sick. She didn't feel feverish, but every time she tried to get out of bed, she was sick. She was also light headed and nauseated. Pauline only felt like this once before, and that was when she had influenza, but she had run a fever that time. There was no sign of her running a fever now.

Pauline asked Homer to go over to her mamma's house and ask her what Pauline should do. Pauline was really scared that there was something seriously wrong, and didn't know if she could even get out of bed to see the local doctor. That was another problem; the doctor had such a large area to cover, that he may not be in the area, and may not be for several days.

Homer didn't even hitch up the horses to the wagon. He saddled Star, their mare, and rode straight over to the Mayfield's. Suzanne was washing clothes in the kitchen. She knew immediately that something was wrong, as she had never seen Homer ride the horses like that before. She met Homer at the front door with a wrinkled forehead, which told Homer of her concern even before she said a word. Homer explained Pauline's condition to his mother-in-law. Before he could even finish describing Pauline's mysterious illness, Suzanne began chuckling. Homer didn't find this situation very funny; in fact, he was very worried about his wife.

Suzanne said she would hitch up her wagon, and be over to see Pauline shortly, but thought that there wasn't really anything to be too concerned about. Homer was confused, but said that he would go tell his wife that her mamma would come to check on her very soon. So just as worried and concerned as before, Homer rode back home.

Suzanne thought she knew what was "wrong" with her daughter, but didn't want to frighten Homer, so she kept her opinion to herself. She knew that when she talked to Pauline, she would know right away if her feelings were correct. The funny thing about all this was, Suzanne, herself, had felt the same way a couple of weeks ago. She had managed to see the doctor, and confirm her suspicions right away.

Suzanne had told Ben right away, and confirmed the diagnosis with the doctor. Ben was so happy; another baby was coming to the Mayfield home. It was a testament of their love for each other. If Pauline hadn't married Homer, and if they hadn't moved into their own little home, things at the Mayfield's might soon be a little over crowded. But instead, they were working on moving Emily upstairs into Pauline's old bed, and make room in their bedroom for the new baby. Dr. Thomas Barnes told Suzanne that she could expect their new little bundle of joy in about seven months. Ben and Suzanne knew that they had time to adjust Emily to the new bedroom. She had only known her little bed in with "mamma and papa". They thought she might object several nights, of her new surroundings; but much to their amazement, Emily adapted very quickly, and liked being by her brothers. Peter and Matthew were not quite so happy about the situation. Emily would often crawl into their bed in the middle of the night, as she had done to their parents many times. Peter and Matthew didn't want to wake their parents, so they would either let her sleep there, or Peter would carefully put Emily back into her own bed.

When Homer had come over, Suzanne had been washing all the baby's clothes she had stored in her trunk at the foot of their bed. She knew she had a long time to get ready, but was actually excited about the new baby, and wanted to get everything washed and put back; also to see what else they might need, see what was worn out, etc. She also washed the blankets and bedding for the cradle. Papa had taken the cradle out to the barn, by his tools and bench, to fix a couple of spindles that had broken over the years of use with their four children. Ben didn't think it would last another child without being mended. Ben had built the cradle when he and Suzanne found out they were expecting Pauline; and now they were expecting another child. Pauline had just left their "nest", and they were just getting used to only having three children in their modest little home, and now that was to be short lived.

* * * * *

When Homer returned home, Pauline was in the outhouse. She was so sick, and didn't know why. It had hit her so suddenly. She could not remember being around anyone that had been ill; although she was still working at Mrs. Kramer's Dress Shoppe. Anything could have come in on the clothes that needed alterations or mending.

Pauline, still trying to figure out why she was sick, had also been at the school the last couple of weeks. She had originally gone to talk to Miss Frederick. Pauline was studying for her teachers' exam. Miss Frederick, Liz, as she

Linda Habeck

asked Pauline to call her, was helping Pauline. They were also becoming friends, and Pauline had agreed that after the exam, she would visit Liz. Liz was renting a room at the *Forette Rooming House*. It was owned by Samuel and Blythe Forette. They were a childless couple that decided to open a rooming house as a way of keeping busy.

Pauline's mind was still wondering, still she could not remember being by anyone that was ill. Where had she gotten this? Yet, she still did not have a fever. What kind of illness could this be? All the time her mind is wondering, she was feeling sicker and sicker.

Homer came looking for Pauline. She could hear him calling her. *"Pauline, where are you?"* He was getting closer and closer, and Pauline didn't want Homer to see her so sick. She tried to compose herself, and came out of the outhouse.

"Homer, what is it?" she inquired on the way out. Her face was still pale, and she was clammy from being sick. Homer grabbed her, and hugged her, reassuring her everything was going to be ok. He explained that her mamma would soon be over to see her, but thought that Pauline would be just fine.

CHAPTER SIXTEEN

❖

The following week Homer was able to track down Dr. Barnes, and made an appointment for Pauline. After their conversation, Dr. Barnes agreed with Mrs. Mayfield, that Pauline was most likely pregnant.

Pauline was slowly getting better, and not quite so sick. She was able to help around the house and land more and more each day. The nausea was lifting. She was still scared; scared that her mother, Homer and Dr. Barnes might be wrong, and scared of the examination with Dr. Barnes.

On the day of Pauline's appointment, Homer hooked up the horses to the wagon, and even made a bed of blankets in the back, in case Pauline became ill on the ride into town. He was so attentive of her as he loved her so much.

Dr. Barnes was in his office, readying it for Pauline's visit. He had doctored her all her life. It was a great feeling to be delivering babies of the "babies" he had delivered.

He wanted the office to feel comfortable for Pauline and other young ladies in her condition. He knew that they were very self conscious, almost to the point of embarrassment. He always had their mothers or another lady of the town, come in with these kinds of examinations. It usually eased the patient's anxieties.

Pauline was able to sit up with Homer all the way to town. Maybe it had been a cold after all, she thought. Then as Homer rounded the last curve heading into town, Pauline felt the nausea flood back, and had to lean over the side of the wagon, and she threw up so hard, she thought she may fall off the wagon.

Homer had a handkerchief in his pocket and handed it to her without even slowing the team and wagon. He wanted to get his new little wife to the doctor's office as soon as possible, to make sure Pauline's mother was right, and nothing else was wrong.

* * * * *

Dr. Barnes had Mrs. Kramer come and sit with Pauline for her examination. Mrs. Kramer held her hand, as Pauline cried. Mrs. Kramer was a Godsend for Pauline, and Pauline told her so. She had never been through anything so terrible. It was such a humiliating exam, but Dr. Barnes confirmed her mothers' suspicions. Pauline was pregnant and should deliver her baby in about eight months, give or take a week or so. This "morning sickness" may or may not go away in a month or so. If it did not go away, Dr. Barnes had a bottle of medicine that should ease the sickness and nausea. He also suggested asking her mother what she did to help with hers.

Dr. Barnes thought it rather funny that Pauline's new sibling should arrive about a month before her own child; the new baby would be an aunt or uncle so soon after birth. They would grow up together, going to school together, etc.

After Pauline's visit with the doctor, Homer took her to see her mother. He figured she might need to talk to her for answers to any questions she had, and to calm any fears she had. He wondered if she could finish her studying for her teacher's exam, and even take the exam. Pauline wanted so much to be a teacher. He hoped she would be able to continue her studies and write the exam. Also, would she have to quit at the Kramer's. She so loved her job, and being able to help with the finances. Homer also appreciated her help.

Homer went to the barn to talk with his father-in-law. What was expected of an expecting husband and father. He knew that Mr. Mayfield had been in that position several times, and what did do for Mrs. Mayfield during these times.

"Papa, what do I do when Pauline's emotions seem to go over the edge? She gets so, well so angry with me over little things, things that never used to bother her."

Ben started to laugh, as he recalled Suzanne's emotions being the same lately. *"Son, bear with her. She isn't sure herself of these emotions."*

"It is the pregnancy son. So it will soon all be over, as soon as that little one arrives. But then she may cry a lot. Suza called it "post partum blues". But that never seemed to last as long as the actual pregnancy did. Thank God."

"Post part em what?"

"It is the name the doc told Suza, it is kind of a depression of not being pregnant. I really do not understand either, except that she cried a lot. But it only lasted a short time, and Suza was back to normal."

"Oh thank you Papa. I thought, I was doing something wrong and Pauline was mad at me. I am scared of being a father myself, sir. I hope I can be half the father, you and my Pop are."

"Thank you son. I am sure you will be fine. You are a wonderful husband to my Pauline. Suza and I are so proud of you. The way you took over that homestead, building my daughter that wonderful home. You and Pauline work so hard on your land. I am sure your folks are just as proud as we are. I am also sure that they are just as excited to become grandparents as Suza and I are. We are just stunned that our littlun and yours, are going to be so close in age. Maybe that is a good thing for Pauline. She can ask her mamma things she is unsure of. Suza really didn't have that luxury when Pauline came. And I am sure Pauline and her mamma will appreciate having each other to confide in. You will both be fine son."

"Thanks Papa. Thanks for all your help and wisdom."

* * * * *

ABOUT THE AUTHOR

I was born and raised in southern Wisconsin but now live on eighty acres of woods in the Upper Peninsula of Michigan—my grandparents homesteaded in the early 1900s. Growing up, my parents, sister, and I "vacationed" on this land in a cabin my parents built.

I was raised with the best of both worlds: city life and country living. I learned to enjoy what nature had to offer, and also the love of reading. At the cabin there wasn't the amenities of home, such as TV. I learned to love to read.

I love waking up every morning to see the deer in my yard. I also enjoy getting on our four-wheeler and riding through the woods, just enjoying nature.

I am married to the love of my life, and we have three kids and nine grandchildren. I love reading to my grand kids and getting them interested in books.

Reading to my kids and grandchildren gave me ideas about writing a book. It is something I have always wanted to give to them, from me: the love of reading.